# MURDER
## AT THE
# CANAVERAL
# DINER

JAY HEAVNER

*Canaveral Publishing*

**All of the author's books can be obtained from Amazon.**
**Braddock's Gold Novels**

*Braddock's Gold*
*Hunter's Moon*
*Fool's Wisdom*
*Killing Darkness*

# Florida Murder Mystery Novels

*Death at Windover*

*Murder at the Canaveral Diner*

## *Dedication*

*To the men and women of the
Brevard Sheriff's Department
serving our county.*

# Acknowledgments

Special thanks to my wife, Vivian, for suggestions ,proofing, support, and editing.

To Dutch Staggs for his helpful ideas and honest review of the unfinished project.

Thanks, William Rowland for the first proofing.

To Dan Mason and Cindy Foley, both fellow

authors, for words of encouragement.

And a special thank you to Wayne Stinnett for his advice and help, above and beyond.

# CHAPTER 1

It was almost high noon when Bill pulled his pickup truck in front of the ancient trailer. Sweat ran down his chest and darkened his uniform. He looked through the vehicle's open window, and he didn't like what he saw. Quietly, he slipped out of the truck, checked his gun, and blackjack in his hip pocket. In his left hand, he held a manila envelope containing the legal paperwork. The fence gate was dummy-locked as he knew it would be, so he let himself in. The yard was a mess. Tall dog fennel grew up everywhere along with the invasive Brazilian pepper bushes.

With stealth, he walked down to the trailer. He heard a menacing growl and stopped. "Hello, K9. How long are we going to continue this charade? I know you better than that. I forgave you for what you did to my truck." The dog growled again, but with little intensity, laid her head down, and closed her eyes. "I thought so." Bill smiled at the dog, opened the door of the screened porch and entered. He turned to the wretch sleeping in the La-Z-Boy chair and shook his head. Bill kicked the chair.

"Wake up," he said firmly.

The wretch shuttered in the chair, opened one bloodshot eye, and said, "Not you again." The eye closed and he resumed sleeping.

Bill had figured this wasn't going to be easy. He waited a moment. The unkempt man began to snore, and Bill kicked the chair harder this time. "I said wake up."

The man jolted in the chair. His head covered with

stringy hair and a week or two beard growth turned toward the voice. His eyes opened. "Oh, you're still here. I thought you were part of a bad dream."

"I'll be your worst nightmare if I don't see some cooperation and respect."

"Okay, Flatfoot. You have my attention. I got to get me a dog. Never know what kind of riff-raff will creep in."

"You got a dog, remember? I helped you get her from the dog pound after your other one died. You remember? The one who pooped and vomited all over my truck?"

"Oh yeah, that dog." He smiled. "That was kinda funny."

"I still hear them call me 'Stinky' behind my back because of you and that little dog. Ain't funny at all, Roger. Not at all."

"She ain't much of a watchdog that's for sure."

"She was when it counted. You'd be pushing up daisies now if it wasn't for her," Bill said.

"I can't argue with that. Why are you bothering me, anyway? I ain't done nothin' wrong for you to come around here unannounced without a warrant and harassin' a peace-loving citizen. Go away."

With all the patience he could muster, Bill said, "As an officer of the law, I'm doing a wellness check on someone who needs it. Do yourself a favor and cooperate."

The wretch seemed to be considering his options. "Oh, alright. What do you want?"

"Well old buddy, I've been worried about you. You're back to where you were when I almost had to use the powers invested in me by the State of Florida and drag you kicking and screaming into the local drunk tank and get you sobered up. You were doing much better when you had a cause, a reason to get up, and now, look at you. You look like hell, like something the cat mauled and dragged in. I hate to see you wasting your life away. You've got so much to offer."

"My life to waste ain't it? After all, I ain't done punishing myself yet, so there."

"What would your wife have to say if she saw you like this?" From Roger's expression, Bill could tell he had the drunken man's attention.

"You like to go for the jugular, don't you?" Bill said nothing and Roger continued, "I don't think she'd be very happy. Have you been talking with Rabbi Katz?"

"Not for a while. Why?"

"When you sent me to see him when we were working the case of the murdered girl found in the pond, he said something like that to me."

"Sounds like the good rabbi. Hey, you got any beer in the frig?"

"Sure do. Get yourself one, but aren't you on duty?"

"I clock myself out one microsecond before the can hits my lips and back in when the can is empty."

"Sounds about right. Get me one too."

"Will do." Bill went into the trailer and soon returned with two cold ones. He gave one to Roger. They popped the tabs and took long sips. "Good and cold and a great price, too," Bill said.

"Yeah, cheap just like you my friend, Chief of Police Bill Kenney. Really now, what brings your sorry carcass over to my humble abode? This ain't no fitness checkup is it?'

"It is, and I do have an ulterior motive."

"Thought so. What is it?"

"As you know, I never undeputized you after we finished the Windover case."

"No, you didn't. Like to got me killed, too."

"So officially, you're still a member of the Canaveral Flats Police Department."

"Guess I am. Get to the point."

"Here. Look at this." Bill handed him the manila envelope. "Open it."

Roger did as he was told. It contained several sheets of paper. He started to read out loud, "Summary. Missy McCoy was murdered September 14, 1980, at the Canaveral Diner Restaurant, Washington Avenue, Titusville, Florida. McCoy was the manager and was closing up late that night alone. She was stabbed 23 times." He stopped. "Just like old Julius Caesar, 23 times."

"Keep reading."

Roger resumed, "23 times post-mortem with a large kitchen knife found at the scene. Subject bled out over a drain. There were signs of sexual trauma, but no semen was recovered. Her body had no defensive wounds. Subject was nude, and her clothing was neatly piled on the floor nearby. Her left nipple had been cut off. No signs of forced entry were found at the establishment. Cause of death could not be determined."

Roger looked at Bill. "This is weird. No signs she put up a fight or any kind of a struggle. Nude, sex, and neatly folded clothing. If it was some kinky sex, you would have expected clothes thrown all over the place. No forced entry to the building and no real clues as to who done it. Why are you showin' this to me?"

"I know you're a firm believer in justice and this woman's killer needs to be brought to justice."

"Agreed, and you want me to find the perp?" Roger said.

"You got it. I know of no one else in the area with your qualifications and tenacity when he puts his mind to it."

"Kind of like Mission Impossible? Here is your mission should you choose to take it and they always do."

"I was hoping you'd look into it."

"Same pay as last time?"

"Guess so."

"Well, thanks for nothing, again." Roger flipped to the next piece of paper and read, "Suspects-Bill Kenney, Jim Odom, unknown." With surprise, Roger said, "You were a suspect? Why?"

"She was my girlfriend until two days before her murder. We had a loud argument when we broke up, so I had motive."

"What about an alibi?"

"None I cared to provide."

Roger looked at him with suspicion. "Who's this Jim Odom?"

"Her ex-husband. It wasn't a pleasant marriage or divorce, but it was short. After a whirlwind romance and marriage, the infatuation died, and they found they hated each other. He had motive, but an alibi."

"What about this unknown person or person of interest?" Roger asked.

"Police securing the scene felt they were being watched by someone or something. They heard noises in the brush behind the restaurant, but could not tell if it was human or animal created."

"So why do you want me to look into this especially if your name was number one on the list?"

"I have my reasons," Bill said.

"And what if I find you done it?"

"I know you'll follow this wherever it leads you."

"You better believe I'll do that, if I take it."

Bill grinned, "I know you will. Gotta go, old buddy. Duty calls. See ya."

"Wait a minute. I need more info on this case."

"I know. You have an appointment with the new cold case unit of the sheriff's department down at their office on Merritt Island at 2 in the afternoon, not tomorrow, but two days from now. Ask for Agent Hernandez."

Roger snarled, "You dog. You dirty, mangy dog. You knew all along I couldn't resist."

"Yup, I was counting on it. And get a shave and haircut and a bath. Put on some clean clothes. You look like a pig, and as a member of the Canaveral Flats Police Department, you must be presentable at the meeting. Don't disappoint me."

Roger swore under his breathe.

"What's that you say?" Bill asked.

"You really don't want to know."

"I thought so. Like I said, I have to go."

"More like you better leave before I chew you a new one," he muttered.

Bill walked to his truck and drove away.

Roger said, "Well dog, looks like I done got suckered into it again. What do you think?"

She opened her eyes, growled deeply and showed her canine teeth. "Yeah K9, that's exactly how I feel right now, but it looks like my curiosity's already in overdrive and runnin' hog wild." He paused. "And old Bill has me just where he wanted, but why?"

# CHAPTER 2

Two days later, Roger pulled his truck into the parking lot of the Brevard County Sheriff's Department off Courtney Boulevard on Merritt Island. The back of his shirt was wet with sweat from the Florida heat in the un-air conditioned truck. The traffic on the Beeline, also known as State Road 528, had been moving well in spite of the tourists heading to the beach and nearby Kennedy Space Center. Crossing the high level bridge over the Indian River, he caught a great view of the huge Vehicle Assembly Building, better known as the VAB, and many of launch towers at the rocket ranch, as the locals often referred to the government area.

A bath and a trim to his overgrown beard and hair at Larry's Barbershop had improved his appearance greatly. He'd do lunch at Umpa's instead of his usual liquid diet, and he was feeling pretty good. Marsha had been there and made a special effort to stop and talk when she could. Running a restaurant with hungry customers coming and going wasn't easy work. A beer at nine in the morning had satisfied his thirst and should hold him over till later after this meeting ended.

He walked across the sweltering parking lot and felt instant relief when he opened the door to the building. "May I help you?" a young woman asked from behind the information counter. She spoke with a heavy Deep South drawl.

"Why, yes. I'm Roger Pyles. I have an appointment at two o'clock with Agent Hernandez."

"Okay, Mr. Pyles. I was told to send you right in. Take the

stairs up to Room 220. Y'all expected."

"Pardon my saying so, but I haven't heard many accents like that around here. Seems like so many people are transplants from someplace up north like me even if I technically live just south of the Mason-Dixon Line."

She smiled. "No, there's not too many of us left. I'm fifth generation Floridian. My folks came down here just after the Civil War. The Space Center was what started the big change around here. This whole area used to be a sleepy place till the '60s when the boom started. Ain't no goin' back now."

"Guess not. What's your name, Miss...?"

"It's Charlotte. I was named after the city. I have sisters Savannah and Florence, and a brother named Jackson."

"All named after cities?"

"No, just us girls. My brother was named after my dad. His name's Jack, and so my brother became Jackson."

"Any others in the family?"

"Just my brothers, Beau and Leroy."

"Good southern names."

"Daddy always wanted a big family. He believed like the Psalmist, 'Blessed is the man whose quiver is full of them.' And my mom's name was Olivia."

"That's definitely not a southern name."

"Nope, unless it's south Italy. Not too many people get to pick and choose their names." She grinned. "Bill said you'd be coming. He described you to a T."

"So you know Bill Kenney?"

"Everybody knows Bill." Her grin grew larger.

Roger wasn't sure he wanted to pursue this line of questioning any longer. "Could you point me to the stairs?"

"It's over there through the oak fire door. At the top of the stairs, turn right. Hernandez's office is second door to the right."

"That should give her a great view of your parking lot, but it'd also be a good place to see a rocket launch."

"It is, but the rooftop is even better. You better get going, or you will be late. Hernandez is a stickler for time."

"Thanks." He bounded up the stairs taking two steps at once. Someone had propped open the fire door at the top of the stairs. He went through the open space and to the second door on the right. It was closed. He rapped on the door. "Come in," a voice said.

Roger did. A woman with light olive skin and dark hair pulled back in a bun sat behind a desk. She was writing on a yellow legal pad. Her white blouse accented her figure. She said, "Please take a seat. Be right with you. Get yourself a cup of coffee if you like while you wait."

"Don't mind if I do." He poured a cup into a white Styrofoam cup, sat back down, and took a sip. "Good coffee." She continued to write as he waited. "I'm here to see Hernandez. I have an appointment about a cold case."

"I know," she said.

"Is he in?"

She stopped writing and looked at him. "I'm Hernandez, Agent Gloria Hernandez."

"Sorry," Roger said surprised. "No disrespect meant."

"None taken. You're not the first one who's done this. I've got a pretty thick skin from working in this line of work with all the testosterone flowing around me daily."

"I expect you would."

She smiled, and he looked at her strangely. "What?" she said. "You seem to have a question."

"Yeah, you look familiar. Have you ever been to Las Vegas?"

"Yes, twice. Once on pleasure and once on business."

"Was the business one a forensics symposium?"

"Yes, it was. How did you know?"

"I was there. You and I spent every free moment we had together, most of it undercover between the sheets and your last name wasn't Hernandez then."

Her eyes grew wide. "Would you shut the door, please?"

Roger did as asked. He wasn't sure what to expect next. He sat back down.

"Yes, I remember," she said. She was trying to keep a straight face, but a look of surprise and maybe even pleasure betrayed her. "I'd almost forgotten. Can we keep this to ourselves?"

"Yeah, I think we can try to keep this professional, though it may be a little awkward at times."

"Agreed. I think I need to do a bit of explaining."

"Whatever you care to share."

She cleared her throat. "I was going through a very rough time in my life. My husband had just left me for another woman. Seems he'd been playing the field the whole time we were married."

"The old story about how you're the last to know," Roger said.

"Exactly. I'd been faithful to that bastard the whole time, and I was angry when we met at the bar after the seminars the first night."

"I remember. It was at the blackjack table, and we hit it right off. You asked me if I was Sam Elliott. I get mistaken for him all the time."

"Yes, I remember that conversation now," she said.

"I have a devil of a time convincing some people I'm not him. Anyway, we were pretty well plastered when we left for my room, and I think we were up about five hundred bucks."

"We were. And I wanted to get even with that son of a bitch cheatin' husband of mine."

"And that's where I came in."

"Yes. Roger, I don't want to make it sound like any gigolo would have worked. I truly enjoyed the time we were able to spend together, and the sex made it even better. You were what I needed, and I'm glad we met."

"Yeah, we did have a good time there. This is gonna complicate it, but I do want to try and keep it professional and only professional as I said."

"Agreed. And the reason for my different name?" she said. "I took my maiden name back after our divorce. So tell me, what's been new with you?"

"Is the nutshell version okay with you?"

"Sure," she said. "Go for it."

"I went on with my training in forensics, helped solve several cases in the area where I live up north, met the girl of my dreams, and married her. The liberal university where I worked as a professor was trying to get me fired because I started to think and ask questions. I was no longer the politically correct good ole boy like them and became persona non grata. They tried to get rid of me. I fought back. It wasn't pretty, and in the middle of this, my wife and our two-year-old son were killed in a car wreck. I was devastated and still not over it now. In the middle of this, the university offered to settle. I had no fight left in me, and I took it. Been living down here for the last year, me and Jim Beam, till Bill Kenney drafted me to help him with the

Windover case."

"Yes," she said. "The case was all over the local news-paper, *Florida Today*. I'm really sorry about your family. I know what it's like to lose a loved one close to you and get screwed over at work. I'm sorry." They said nothing for a moment. She asked, "Was the information in the paper correct?"

"For the most part, but they left a lot out and had to hide some the truths in plain sight among a bunch of gobbledygook. There were some 'national security' issues I'd rather not go into. Probably better if you don't know."

"Probably right. Sounds about right with the news media today. I ran into some situations like that down in Miami."

Roger said, "Yeah, that's right."

"You spilled your guts. Now it's my turn to clear some air. Seems we were enjoying ourselves too much in Vegas and never got around to talking about our personal lives. My father and mother escaped from Cuba. The rest of the family's still there just getting by in that Communist hellhole. They were Jews that left Spain during the Spanish Inquisition, and when Castro came to power, they saw the writing on the wall. They knew it was time to pick up roots and leave again for them. They couldn't have any kids, and I was adopted in Miami. My adopted mom died when I was a teenager. She just never woke up one morning – died in her sleep. I don't know who my real parents are or were. Maybe one day I'll look into it.

She continued, "My adopted dad was one of the first Cubans on the police force in Miami. The old guard didn't like him or the fact Miami was becoming mostly Cuban, but they needed him because he was bilingual. Mom and Dad always spoke English in front of me. They felt it was important to adapt to their new home, so I never learned much Spanish. He got me into the police force and shortly afterwards was killed in a shootout with the cocaine cowboys on a highway in busy

Miami. He was in the wrong place at the wrong time, and it cost him his life. I got my sense of justice from him. The bad guys have to go down, pay for their crimes."

"Guess we're alike on that," Roger said. "I've found a bunch of things in my work I wish I hadn't involving human depravity and corruption."

"Tell me about it. Miami has it all and more. Makes you sick at your stomach sometimes. They've even come out with a TV show recently, called appropriately, 'Miami Vice,' but the show's tame compared to some of what I've heard and seen."

Roger said, "You would know. Probably be more shows about all that went on."

She said, "About the same time, the Feds were looking and finding mega corruption in the police force down there. When I finished my training in police work and forensics, I wanted to get the hell out of Dodge before I got tainted by simply being there. Brevard County was looking to start a forensics unit, and I'm it so far. I'm overwhelmed, understaffed, and underfunded, but what else is new with police work?"

"You forgot unappreciated."

"Yes, that too, and a woman with a Latino name doesn't help with this crowd."

"How are they treating you here?" Roger asked.

She shrugged. "Better than Miami. It's not all bad. Times are changing."

"So what have you got to show me for records on the cold case Bill sent me here about?'

"Old Bill, he's a charmer."

"That he is, and a little scoundrel thrown in for good measure." A little laugh escaped his lips.

"I had that feeling. I've learned to read people really well,

Roger."

"So what's your impression of me today?"

"Good heart, a believer in justice, and a man who would like to escape the burdens of his life or conquer them."

"You read all that from our talk here?"

"Yes, and some things that are coming back to me from our time in Vegas," she said. "I believe you were a very good father to your child."

"I wish I'd died instead of him and his mom."

"I believe you would." She stopped. "You ready to see the rest of the evidence on what's been called the Missy McCoy case?"

"Sure. What's you got?"

"Not near as much as I'd like. My general impression is a very casual investigation was done of the crime. They did secure the area as is procedure, but forensics could have been done better. We have a few pictures, and I think there was more paperwork done. There seem to be gaps like some things were lost or possibly removed from the evidence before I got here. Seems like anyone wearing a badge or having clearance could just walk in, and no records of the coming and going were ever kept."

Roger's eyebrows rose. "Woo. That's not at all good. If word about this were to get out, every defense lawyer would have an orgasm with that information."

"True. It is what it is, and we'll have to deal with it, bitter or sweet. Take a look at what we have." She handed him a large manila envelope which he opened.

"Okay, let's see what we have here. I've seen the summary before. It was the teaser Bill gave me to draw me in, but not the photos. Someone had a lot of pent-up hatred for her."

"Twenty three stab wounds post-mortem. I've seen worse, but I agree. What else do you see, Roger?"

"Nude and the report said there was possible sexual assault, correct?

"Yes, also postmortem and no semen. We think the perp wore a rubber."

"No sign of forced entry into the building. My impression is this was planned out in advance."

"We're on the same page."

"She's missing her left nipple. Looks like it was cut off also post-mortem?"

She nodded. "That was my conclusion also."

"Souvenir to keep and remember?"

"My thought also."

"This helps, but it seems there should be more records than this."

"The Deputy who discovered her, a fellow named Miller who's now retired, should be able to provide more information. Evidence on the case has disappeared in the last five years. It may have just been misplaced, I hope, but I fear the worse. The evidence room was a mess when I arrived here, all disorganized and very poor security. Miller moved some place up north. I've been trying to find where and reach out to him."

"Good. When you call him, give him a heads up on me helping with the case I'd like to talk to him, in person if possible. A phone call would work, but face to face is better. Could you see if that could be arranged?"

"I'll do that and would you like to see the Canaveral Diner? It could help you picture the scene of the crime and how it went down."

Roger said, "Yeah, please do both of those things and make it ASAP. My curiosity is up, and it needs satisfied."

A little smile came to her face. She went to say something, but held back at the last moment. Her face went neutral, and she said, "I'll do that."

"Do you have anything more?"

"No, that's about it, but here's my business card so you can contact me when you need to."

"I'll do that. Thanks for the coffee. Can I take these with me?" he said.

"They're copies. Just follow the standard procedures for evidence."

"Will do. Hope we can find who done this. Not much to go on, but you never know where one little seemingly insignificant detail will lead."

"I can see why Bill wanted you for this case, Roger."

"I've known him since we were kids back in West Virginia. With Bill, there's the obvious face value, but often there's another motive or motives not so apparent."

"One reason he has the reputation he does," she said.

"Yup. I'd better go. Thanks for the coffee. I'll be in touch as needed."

"Roger, Bill gave me your phone number, and I'll contact you about the Canaveral Diner visit and Miller as soon as I have something."

"Okay, I'm counting on it. Bye."

Roger got up and left the room. Deputy Hernandez sat at her desk. That was about the last person she ever expected to see. She put on latex gloves, got a paper sack, and walked to the trash can. Carefully, she picked up the discarded coffee cup and put it in a paper bag. She wondered. There was only one way to know for sure.

# CHAPTER 3

It was 9:30 p.m. when Roger pulled in to the parking lot of the Canaveral Diner in Titusville, Florida. The diner was easy to find at the east end of State Route 50 where it t-boned US 1. Roger looked across the broad Indian River Lagoon and could see several structures lit up against the horizon. The massive and tall Vehicular Assembly Building was easy to identify as were Launch Pads, 39A and 39B, where the civilian-run Space Shuttle was launched. He could see several other tall buildings further south on the Cape Canaveral Air Force Station. The US Military had their launch facilities there. The two agencies were separate, but often cooperated on programs.

He stepped out of his truck. The stiff breeze from the river blew at his hair and kept hungry mosquitoes at bay, more or less. One buzzed at his ear, and he swatted it. This was his first time to the Canaveral Diner, and he was impressed by the outside. The building was square with lots of glass on the sides that faced the Space Center and the highways. It had the shiny chromed metal exterior he'd expected and lots of neon strip lights, red, white, and blue, circling the top of the building. A huge sign sprang from the roof. "Canaveral Diner," it said in huge letters. Below that in smaller print he could hardly read said, "Best Grub in the Universe."

Roger looked at his watch, 9:45. He wondered where Hernandez was. She'd told him to be here no later than 9:15. He'd been worried about being late. Now she wasn't here. A truck he recognized pulled off the highway and parked next to him. Roger looked at Canaveral Flats Chief of Police Bill Kenney.

"Hey flatfoot, aren't you a little out of your jurisdiction?" asked Roger.

"You were expecting Agent Hernandez?" Bill said.

"I was. She's a lot better looking than you, old buddy. What are you doing here anyway?"

"She couldn't make it. She was heading out the door when she got a call. Seems someone stumbled onto some bones, probably human, out near the Ag Center out on Highway 520 and she had to go there. Called me and asked me if I'd cover for her so here I am. If you're disappointed, suck it up, buttercup."

"You can be a real pain, you know, Bill?"

"Yup. You can always depend on me. Let's get to work. Quit your yammering, and let's head over yonder."

"Alrighty. They're expecting us aren't they?" he said as they walked toward the building.

"Yup. We can grab a bite to eat if you want. They're closing soon, and we can have the place to ourselves while they clean up. The manager and owner is here and has agreed to stay till we're done. Hernandez said he wants to see this crime solved. Seems he's considering selling out to a gas station chain."

They walked in the building and sat down. A blond haired woman who sat with her back to them was the only other customer. A door opened from the back, and a portly man fiftyish came out and went to the men. "Hey, Bill. What's you doin' here? I was expecting some young Hispanic lady named Hernandez. No way you fit that bill, Bill."

"Something came up, and she asked me to help out. Pete, this is Roger Pyles. He's been asked to look into this case. Tell him anything you know about what happened here five years ago."

Pete stuck out his hand, and Roger took it. "Pleased to

meet you, Lt. Pyles," Pete said.

"And pleased to meet you also, Pete....? What's the last name?"

"Bertella."

"Good Italian name if I ever heard one. And it's Mister Pyles. Right Chief Kenney?"

Bill looked surprised by Roger's question. "Yup, that'll work for me. Work for you, Roger?"

"Guess it will have to for now." He gave Bill a dirty look. "So tell me, Pete, how'd you end up in Florida and owning this diner?"

"My dad had a diner up in Pittsburgh downtown near the Golden Triangle area not too far from where Three Rivers Stadium is now."

"Go Steelers," Roger said.

"Pirates too," Pete said. "It's the usual story. He was tired of the winters, and when the state needed to build a four-lane highway right through his business, he held out till the price was right, sold out, and purchased this piece of property dirt cheap when Titusville had more mosquitoes and alligators than people. He bought the last prefab diner Mountain View Diner Company made and had it trucked down here from New Jersey just about the time the Space Center was really starting up. People would jam this place whenever there was a launch. I can remember many days we were open 24/7 when there was a delay. We prayed for them and cursed them. We made lots of money but were dog tired and thankful when the bird finally did launch. The old diner built on a trolley car frame wasn't big enough and was falling apart so in 1978, we had the old place torn down and this new, modern diner was built. Glad we did. What do you think of it?"

Roger said, "It's very nice. Sure a lot bigger and fancier

than the originals." Bill nodded in agreement.

Peter said, "We went whole hog in the use of stainless steel, neon, mirrors, and ceramic tile. You guys want anything before I close?"

"Yeah," they said in unison.

"You first," Roger said.

"Thanks," Bill said. "About time you showed some respect for your boss."

Roger gave him a sarcastic look. "Whatever."

"Okay, now we got that straight, how 'bout getting me two eggs over easy and two strips of bacon well done and an English muffin."

"Got it," Pete said. He looked at Roger. "And you, Roger?"

"I have one of what he's having. Sounds good, but make my bacon still limber, not stiff, okay?"

"Gotcha," Pete said. "I'll have it out in a jiffy. We close in ten minutes to the public. When you guys are done, I can show you the place, and you guys can try to figure out what happened."

"Okay," Bill said. Pete left and went into the kitchen.

The lady who'd been sitting got up to leave. As she passed the men, she stopped. "Well, hello Bill. Long time no see. Where have you been keeping yourself?"

Bill turned to the woman. A look of surprise came to his face followed by a knowing smile. He seemed taken back. "Why, hello Shirley. It's been a long time. Guess our paths have just not crossed. It's been a while. How you been doing?"

"Oh, life's had its ups and downs. You did know I'm separated from B. J. and filed for divorce?"

"Yeah, I heard it through the grapevine."

"It was a hard decision to make, but I think it will be better in the long run," she said and looked at Roger. "And who's your friend?"

Bill said, "Where are my manners? Shirley, this is Roger Pyles. He's helping with the investigation on the murder which took place right here five years ago."

"Roger Pyles," she said." It's good to meet you. Are you by chance the same Roger Pyles who the local paper mentioned on the Windover dig and also the Stiltsville fire?"

"Yup, that'd be me."

"Thought it might be." She looked at Bill and said, "Bill and me go way back."

A knowing look came to his face. "Yeah, it's been probably a decade or more since we first met. Roger, Shirley was married to B. J. Harden. He was a county commissioner, and our paths crossed often. That's how I met her. Lotta water passed under the bridge since then, Shirley."

"Yes, there has." She said, "Some bitter, some sweet, and some polluted."

"That pretty much sums it up."

She started to say something, but the door to the kitchen clanked open, and she stopped. Her eyes were on Bill, and Roger noticed him mouth the word, "No." Roger turned his eyes back to the approaching Pete. Something had happened here, but he wasn't sure what.

Pete said, "Guys, we're totally out of bacon. The supplier said there was some kind of recall and we won't have any till tomorrow. Would two hickory smoked ham steaks work for you?"

"Sure thing," Roger said.

"Yeah, I haven't had one of those in a month of Sundays. Make sure it's well done," Bill said

"Mine too," Roger said. Pete gave a thumbs up and disappeared back into the kitchen.

"Guess I better be going," Shirley said. "Give me a call, Bill and don't let it be so long as it has been." She directed her eyes to Roger. "Good to meet you, Roger and if there's any way I can help, please feel free to get in touch. Enjoy yourselves. I sure did. Bye." And with that, she was off.

"Bye," Bill said.

"Please to meet you, Shirley," Roger said. "I'll remember that."

She turned slightly as she left. She had a coy smile on her face but tried not to let it show. She said no more and left.

The two men said nothing for a moment. Bill cleared his throat. "I ah, I got in touch with Miller. He agreed to meet, but he wants it at his house, and he would like both of us there."

"Wonder why?" Roger asked.

"He said he could be more candid that way and wanted to see me again. He's an old friend."

"Okay. When?"

"We leave tomorrow morning about ten. It'll take eight hours to drive there. He said he had lots of room and invited us to stay the night. I said I'd run it by you. I had to rearrange some things here, and I knew you weren't doin' nothin' productive, so I said yes for you too, Roger. We'd come at a time that was convenient for him."

"Well thanks, old buddy. You sure know how to hurt a guy. Not doin' nothin' productive, huh. For all you knew, I could have had an audience with the Queen."

"Crown Royal, I could believe."

"Okay, maybe a doctor appointment."

"Who?"

"Oh, don't get started on that again."

"I won't. Besides, Who's on first."

Roger rolled his eyes in mocking disgust. The kitchen door sprang open, and Pete came out carrying two steaming hot plates of food. He placed them on the table and said, "Enjoy fellows. It's on the house."

"We can't take that," Roger said.

"But I insist," Pete said. "It's the least I can do to help you finding out who killed Missy."

"Well, thanks. I wasn't expecting it," Bill said.

"Enjoy boys," Pete said. "I should be about done cleaning up by the time you've finished that off. I'll help you in any way I can. Just let me know."

"Sure thing. Thanks," Bill said.

It only took a few minutes for the two men to wolf down the hearty meal.

Roger had a satisfied look on his face and said, "Okay, Sherlock. Where do we start?"

"Isn't it obvious, Watson? In the beginning," Bill emphasized, "In the beginning. The game is afoot."

# CHAPTER 4

The two men turned their heads as the lights on the big neon sign by the road, and the lights in the parking lot went out. Pete came out from the kitchen and locked the front door. He slipped into the booth next to Roger and said, "You guys really think you can crack this cold case after all this time has gone by?"

"We hope so," Bill said. "And I know of no better person able to get to the heart of the matter than Roger. He was a forensics and archaeological professor up north and knows his way around this stuff. It ain't his first rodeo. He helped the police solve several cases while living there."

"Missy was a great worker. She left a big hole that was difficult to fill, but somehow you manage," Pete said.

"Thanks for the compliment, Bill. Hope I can live up to that reputation," Roger said.

"First thing first," Bill said. "This could be complicated for me so I'll show my cards from the beginning. It would be nice if I could stay out of this for reasons I'll mention, but I can't. I think you know I was a suspect in this. Missy and I were romantically involved, and we had a loud breakup two days before she was killed here. Much of the paperwork from this case seems to be missing or lost. Roger, you don't know this, but I was one of the first people to get here about 4:30 that morning. Pete found her dead on the floor, called it in, Deputy Miller was first on the scene, secured the area, and called for help. I heard the call and responded as I was in the area."

"And what were you doing in the area at that hour of the morning?" Roger asked.

"I'd rather not say. You're gonna have to figure that out," Bill said.

"You know I will," Roger said.

Bill said, "As I remember it, the lights were on low in the dining area. The front door was open, and crime tape was across the entrance. Pete was sitting at the bar trying to drink a cup of coffee. He was very distraught. I was in civilian clothes and identified myself as a policeman. Pete said that a female employee was dead in the kitchen. Is that about how you remember it, Pete?"

"That's it in a nutshell. I'll add anything more I can remember I think could be important."

Bill said, "You do that. I went into the kitchen and found Deputy Miller. He knew me and asked me if I was here to help. I said yes, and we made sure the area was secure and put crime tape over the back door which was locked. Pete, was the door locked and closed when you arrived?"

Pete said, "It was. I unlocked the front door, came in, turned on the lights, and went to the kitchen to get ready for breakfast. I saw Missy lying on the floor naked. Her eyes were glazed over. I knew she was dead. I touched her. She was cold. And yes, the door was closed and locked. Then I called the cops."

Roger asked, "Did you move her or anything in the building?"

Pete said, "No, the only thing I did was put on a pot of coffee. I knew I needed it and figured the cops would want some when they got here. I sat down in a booth and waited. The coffee had just stopped perking when Deputy Miller arrived. I met him at the door and took him back to the kitchen. Though I was shaking like a leaf, he was calm as a cucumber. He checked for a pulse and found none. Later, he told me he just did that to make sure. He saw the glazed over eyes and knew she was dead."

"He asked me if this was how I found her and I said, 'Yes.' He asked if I had moved her or anything in the kitchen. I said, 'No.' At that point, he got on his radio, reported what he had found, and asked for backup help. It was going to be a long morning for everyone. Bill showed up soon afterward. They secured the area. I got everyone coffee and sat the cups on a table by the window. We sat down, and they asked a lot of questions.

"Were the doors all locked?" Roger asked.

"Yes," Pete said. "They found a key in the rear door lock. I don't know if the investigators ever figured out if it had any significance or not."

Roger nodded. "That is interesting. I'll look into that. Sometimes little details like that can make or break a case. What else, Pete?"

"Two other cops arrived about that time, one a Titusville cop and one a county Mountie. Can't remember their names. Bill, do you remember?"

"I do. The Titusville cop was a rookie named Schumer, totally useless. It was his first murder. After he saw the body, he turned green and threw up in a kitchen sink. What a mess. We sent him out to his car, and he spent the next hour sitting in his patrol car with the driver's door open with his head between his legs throwing up about every fifteen minutes. Not sure he's around anymore. The deputy's name was Yates. Good guy you can depend on."

Roger said, "I think I know him. Is that the same guy who pulled a gun on us at the Port St. John boat dock?"

"It is, but remember, we were going 90 mph down US 1 in my old truck and there was a car burning up at the boat dock that early morning."

"Yeah, I remember. Someone had just tried to shoot me dead, and we were after him."

"Yup," Bill said. "It's also the same deputy who should have thrown you and Tom Kenney in jail for being drunk and disorderly."

Roger said, "You forgot resisting arrest."

Bill smiled, "I didn't forget. Call it selective memory to protect the guilty." He paused. "Just be thankful he owned me some favors and called me and didn't take you guys in."

Roger grimaced, "Yeah, Tom's wife blew a head gasket when she found out. Glad there was a thousand miles between us."

"Why was that?" Pete asked.

"Well," Bill said, "Tom's wife, Sarah, is Navajo and wanted to do grave bodily harm to dear ole Roger for his instigation of the confused fiasco that night."

"Yeah, think I'll stay away from her for the foreseeable future till and if she calms down," Roger said.

"She wanted to turn his private parts into some, shall we say, personal accessories like the Indians did with bull buffalos," Bill said.

"Sounds like someone I would want as a friend and not an enemy," Pete said.

The two men across from them nodded in agreement. Roger said, "Looks like I may need to talk to Yates about this."

"Don't forget to thank him for not running your sorry slobbering self in that night," Bill said.

"I will," Roger replied and then mumbled, "And thanks to you, too."

Bill's eyes widened. He looked at Pete and said, "Did you

hear something? I'm not sure I did."

Pete picked up on what was going on. "I believe I did hear something, but it was very garbled. Maybe if we're lucky, it will come around again."

"Okay, THANK YOU, BILL! Now, are you happy?" Roger said.

"Shocked," Bill said. "Didn't think I'd hear those words. Maybe you were worth saving."

Roger gave Bill his best Sam Elliott irritated look and said, "Now, can we get back to the investigation? Pete, is there anything more you would like to add now?"

"Not really. The policemen that were here took it and ran with it. I was pretty much a forgotten bystander looking out the window and watching the young useless cop Schumer puking over and over."

Roger said, "Okay, I may need to talk with you again as questions come up. Where can I reach you?"

"Just call the restaurant. I'm here most of the time. Not sure if I own it or it owns me," Pete said. "Be great to make a new start while I still can. I've seen so many people put off plans till they retire and then something happens to one of them or the other. They make plans to do this or that and then one dies or gets sick and it never happens. Me, I'm getting out while I can and healthy enough to enjoy life."

Bill asked, "So what are your plans?"

Pete said, "Well, me and the misses are going to travel for a while and then I'll golf a lot to keep out of her hair."

Roger said, "Seems like a plan for a while. Anything after that? Seems like a short-term plan only."

"I've thought about that," Pete said. "I could always open up another diner. Even though it takes up lots of time, I'm a people person, and I'm not sure I'll be happy with all the free time. It's great to make people happy with a great meal, and then share what's going on in their lives."

"Sounds like a plan," Roger said. He looked at Bill. "Yates should be easy to find and talk to." Bill nodded. "You have any idea where and when we can see this Deputy Miller fellow?"

"I do," Bill said. "He's retired, moved to Greenville, South Caroline, and we're gonna see him tomorrow."

"What?" Roger said.

"I contacted him for you. He's leaving for Pennsylvania in three days, and we're leaving for Greenville tomorrow morning early."

"What?" Roger said. "Who's gonna feed my dog while we're gone?"

"It's all taken care of," Bill said. "I got your neighbor Lester lined up to take care of K9."

"Sounds like I've been shanghaied. Anything else I need to know?"

"Yeah, you need a bath and a real haircut, and your breath smells like a north end of a horse going south. Clean up your act if you want to get along with Miller. He used to be a drill instructor for the Marines before he joined the Sheriff's Department. A lifer he was and goes strictly by the book. You need to look good if you want to talk to him."

Roger protested, "But I had a bath and got my beard and hair trimmed."

Bill shook his head. "Use soap this time and take a real shower, not a quick rinse this time. And get your hair and beard cut, not trimmed around the edges. The work is Miller's hard core, so you need to cut it seriously. Got that?"

Roger said, "Okay, I'll look professional."

"Good, we want to make a good first impression," Bill said.

Pete said, "You boys figure out the details on your trip. I have to get back to the kitchen. We won't be ready for our next meal if I'm not helping. Roger, good luck. Find the bastard that did this. Missy needs justice. I'm counting on you. You know where to find me when you need me. Bye." He got up and disappeared through the double swinging doors into the kitchen.

"You got it all figured out, don't you, Bill?"

"Somebody has to, old buddy, till you're back to running with the big dogs again."

Roger's eyes shot bullets across the table and he said, "Be glad I married a good Christian woman and her influence is still with me. God rest her soul. I'm biting my tongue and not repeating the many four-letter words I'm thinking about you now."

"I wish I could have met her, Roger. She sounds like she was a wonderful woman."

"She was, and our son looked just like her. God, how I miss them."

The two men said nothing for a moment. "What time tomorrow are we leaving for Greenville?" Roger asked.

"Ten o'clock in the morning. That'll give you time to get a real haircut. Larry's opens; I think seven or seven-thirty. Be there when they open."

"Okay, I'll see you then, ole buddy." Roger emphasized the last two words.

The men got up, left the diner, and walked to their trucks. Bill said, "Thanks for cleaning up your act somewhat, ole buddy. You got more to go."

Roger smiled at him sardonically. "Right," he said and then drove away.

Bill sat in his truck and stared out across the Indian River to the buildings at Kennedy Space Center. *The die had been cast. There was no turning back now. It was go for launch.*

# CHAPTER 5

The next morning at 10 a.m.

Bill pulled up to the gate at Roger's humble abode. There was little traffic on Canaveral Flats Boulevard, but that was normal even for a workday. Maybe someday as the area grew, this unpaved washboard road would live up to its name. He liked it the way it was even with the big holes that filled with water after a rainstorm. It cut down on speeders and kept outsiders out. He'd regularly seen people with out of state tags stop at Miller's Store. Some got directions from Fred. Others just turned around, and high tailed it back to "civilization."

It made his job easier as the only town cop. Most of the town's residents had trucks with high clearance, but a few drove all-wheel-drive cars that usually could make it through except for the very worst of places on the very worst of days.

The gate was dummy locked as usual, so Bill let himself in. He could see Roger asleep on the screened in porch in his new La-Z-Boy chair. The bullets from the assassin's gun had destroyed the last one and nearly gotten Roger killed. Bill hoped this case would go smoother, but you never know. Police work always had an element of danger in it. Like most law officers, Bill had a desire to serve and try to make the world a little better. With time, he found the job was mostly routine and even boring, but it also had its 5% of sheer terror.

He drove up the path and got out. Immediately, he heard a familiar growl. "K9," Bill whispered. "It's good to see you too.

Looks like you're still mad at me, or is that your way of saying 'Hello?'"

The dog gave him a 'whatever' look and went back to sleep. Bill saw K9's water and food bowl were both full. He wondered if Roger had done this, but doubted it. A quick look at Roger told him Roger had taken some of his advice. His hair was cut, his beard was shaved, and he smelled of Old Spice cologne, not B.O. The familiar Sam Elliott walrus mustache was back. Seemed he had bathed also. Bill wondered if Roger's shower was cold. Roger frequently would forget to get a tank of propane when it ran out. He could have lit the water heater each time he needed it, but usually, Roger left the pilot light on. Roger said it kept the mechanism from rusting up, but as often as he ran out of gas and did without, Bill couldn't see how it made any difference. Whatever.

"Hey, Rip Van Winkle, it's time to rise and shine. Road trip, remember?" Bill shouted.

Roger opened one eye, looked at Bill and said, "I ain't feeling so good. I got a headache."

Bill saw an empty whiskey bottle nearby, but said nothing.

Roger snarled, "I got to get me a dog." Bill opened his mouth to speak, but Roger cut him off. "I know. I know. I do have a dog, a good one, too. She's welcome here as long as she keeps the riff-raff out and growls at you."

Bill said, "Did you feed K9?"

"No, must have been Lester."

"Does she growl at Lester?"

"No, Lester ain't riff-raff like some people who have been known to disturb my sleep and drink my beer. Know anyone else who fits that description?"

Bill smiled and stroked his chin. "Oh, about half the

people in Canaveral Flats or more."

Roger looked at Bill and said, "You don't want to hear what I'm thinking."

"Probably not, ole buddy. Remember, I'm the closest thing you've got for a true friend in this world."

"Thanks. You would have to remind me of that. You really know how to make my day."

Bill smiled, "It's always good to be appreciated. Looks like you took some of my advice. Got your stuff ready for the trip?'

"Yeah, I knew I wouldn't be in any shape or want to do it this morning. Got it all in a little day pack wheelie thing I got at a thrift store near Larry's Barbershop. I'm ready as I will be."

Larry's wife, Linda, cut your hair?"

"Yeah, she did."

"Looks like her work."

Roger got out of his chair, stood, and looked at the full dog bowls. "Yup, looks like Lester has been here already, or the good fairies have visited."

Bill said, "I'd bet on Lester. Good fairies usually avoid this neighborhood. Too many big dogs. Now, Lester on the other hand, has made friends with many of the dogs in the area. They used to be a real problem for him when he wanted to cut the lawns for the owners when they were at work, but he discovered if he feeds them doughnuts beforehand, they leave him alone."

"Doughnuts, huh? Bet you know about doughnuts."

"Hey, cool the jokes about cops and doughnuts. Remember, officially you're one, too."

"Guess you're right on that," Roger said.

"Oh, and FYI, Lester used to be a scout in World War II. He got several medals, but he doesn't talk about the war much. Too many bad memories."

"There's a lot of guys like that. They don't open up on the war subject. Just too painful."

"Agree, get your stuff and we'll be off," Bill said.

"Okay. It'll only take a minute or two."

Roger went inside and soon returned with a backpack with wheels. It had a TMI label on the outside that Bill noted. "Where'd you get that thing?" Bill said and pointed at the backpack.

"A church thrift store near the barbershop?"

"Was it the Catholic one or the Baptist's shop?"

"I don't know, Bill. How many are there?"

"A bunch. Seems every church and community service organization from people needs to animal needs to environmental needs has one."

"I'll keep that in mind. Seems like good places to shop with reasonable prices and help the area needs too."

"I do almost all my shopping for clothes there."

Roger grinned, "I never would have guessed. I thought you went dumpster diving for what those places threw out."

"Very funny, Roger. Now you know why you have so few friends."

"By the way, what's TMI anyway?" Roger asked.

"TMI stands for Teen Missions International. They're located over on Merritt Island, a Christian group. They have a summer camp, a boot camp they call it, before they send teens out on mission trips all around the world."

"Interesting. Ready to go?"

"Sure, let's hit the road like sheep dung."

"Roger curled up his lip. Sheep dung? You usually use more colorful language."

"Roger, I told you I was trying to clean up my act. Now, do you want to argue about what comes out of the back of a sheep or go?"

"Let's go, and I know what comes out of the hindquarters of sheep and other animals, politicians."

"No argument there. Let's go."

They hopped in Bill's truck and were soon on the road. Roger knew they were heading for South Carolina, but he wondered where this investigation would be heading, especially with one of the two prime suspects sitting next to him and driving. He had mixed feelings on how this would turn out.

# CHAPTER 6

Roger opened his eyes and looked around. "Where are we, Bill?"

"Almost to St. Augustine. It's about time you woke up, Rip Van Winkle."

"Told you I wasn't feeling good. I can't believe I slept that long and then the first thing I saw was you, Bill. Wasn't sure if I was still asleep or not. Like a nightmare you can't wake up from. What a fright."

"Very funny, ole buddy. You're making me think twice about helping you."

Roger grunted and gave Bill his best Sam Elliott cowboy annoyed look. "I'm hungry and I gotta pee. How about stopping? Know any place close with good eats?"

"Sure do, and you're in luck. They serve everyone, even grumpy old men like you."

Roger growled, "You're a good one to talk. How far is it?"

"Next exit. About five miles. Can your bladder wait that long?"

"Yeah, I think so."

"Just checkin'. Sometimes it's a long way between pit stops on some of our highways and other times the urge can sneak up on us kind of sudden as we get older."

"Yeah, I know what you're saying about that."

Bill said, "I've seen some embarrassing things along the roads. Usually guys, but sometimes women and kids. I remember coming back from Orlando on 528 better known as the Bee-line. As I took the left exit and got past the long overpass, I saw a white Jeep Cherokee parked on the shoulder up ahead. Those things have a very high road clearance as you well know. I saw a set of adult legs I found out as I passed them that belonged to the momma and next to her was a poor little girl squatting and her butt exposed to God and everyone. A yellow stream ran about 20 feet past the back of the vehicle. Poor thing really had to go.

"I sometimes umpire ball games for the young kids at Fay Park Ballpark in Port St. John. It's interesting seeing the youths learn the fundamentals of baseball. It can be quite amusing at times too. I remember one game where a boy about six just wiped it out at second base and made a big puddle next to the bag. He stepped off the bag, and the coach told the boy on his team to tag him. He did, and I called the other boy out. I think he learned two lessons that day."

"Yeah, don't pee on the field and stay on the bag," Roger said.

"Yup. Another time, a little girl about seven was playing ball. Her coach was pitching to her. She hit the ball and ran to first. She no more than got there, when she began to jump up and down on the bag, holding herself, and yelling to the top of her lungs so everyone in the park and maybe even Almighty God far away in Heaven could hear, 'I gotta pee!'

"So as the umpire, what did you do, Bill?"

"I called time and said to the coach, 'Coach, the little girl has to pee. What are we gonna to do?' She rolled her eyes, got another girl to be a pinch runner, and the first little girl ran with her hands on her crotch across the infield over third base and disappeared into the bathrooms just off the side of the field. It was funny. Everyone in the stands was roaring with laughter, and it only got louder as word was circulated that the pee girl was the coach's daughter. It was a long time out before we could get back to the game. Little kids have no filter when it comes to letting you know about their bodily needs."

Roger looked at Bill and said, "Ole buddy, would you please quit talking about peeing? Now I got to go worse. I may have to tie it in a knot to keep from wetting myself."

"Would tweezers and a magnifying glass help with that chore?"

"Shut up and hurry, please," Roger said.

"If it was longer, you could hang it out the window and go. People behind us would just think I was spraying water on the windshield to clean it."

"Shut up! Please hurry before I do something rash."

Bill smiled and said no more. Three minutes later, they pulled into the parking lot of a fast food restaurant. As soon as the truck stopped, Roger jumped out and literally ran into the building. Bill locked his vehicle and went inside. He sat at an empty booth and waited. Roger appeared from the restroom with a look of relief on his face. He slid into the booth across from Bill. He asked, "Don't you have to go?"

Bill said, "I went at the rest stop about 30 miles ago. You were sleeping so peacefully, I let you sleep. No point in waking you and hear you growling like a bear."

"Wish you had. I growl worse when waking up and I gotta pee and relief's miles down the road. Guess I could have relieved myself in your truck like my dog did."

"Now Roger, you know that ain't even funny. They still call me nasty things behind my back because of you and that dog of yours. Maybe you need to ride in the back like I made you and the dog after the accident in the cab."

Roger smiled, "You remember what happened then, don't you? Things went from bad to worse."

"You would have to remind me. I liked to never get all that gooey crap out of the truck bed. Maybe that wasn't my best idea, but I'm just glad she didn't explode like that in the cab."

"Probably right. It all worked out, but makes for an interesting and funny story."

"Maybe now, but it wasn't funny when it happened."

"So, I never been in a Chick-fil-A before. What's good on the menu?" Roger said.

"Chick-fil-A's one of the great things about the South. Maybe someday they'll be everywhere in America, but now they're not in Yankeeland, just Dixie. Try the Number 1, chicken biscuit, waffle fries, and a drink."

"Waffle fries? What's that?"

"Trust me. You'll like them. Have I ever led you wrong?"

Roger grinned. "Do you want me to give you a straight answer on that?"

"Probably not, but trust me on this. You're in for a treat."

The two men both ordered a Number 1 with coffee. It was served to them quickly, and they sat down to eat.

Bill watched as Roger unwrapped his chicken sandwich. He took a bit, looked at Bill, and nodded his head. Roger said, "You're right. This is good."

"I told you, you could trust me. Try the waffle fries."

Roger bit into them. "Right again. Very tasty." He took a sip of the coffee. "Um, this is good too. Just like I like it."

"I knew you'd like this place. It's one of my favorites when I travel. Ain't none in Brevard County yet, but I've heard rumors now and then of one of these openings up back home.'

"I hope they do. They've won me as a customer."

The hungry boys finished their meal quickly, got a refill

on the coffee, and were soon back on the highway traveling north on I 95.

Bill commented, "Have you ever been to St. Augustine?"

"Can't say I have."

"You're missin' so much. Oldest place in America. Interesting old town area. Ponce de Leon was looking for the Fountain of Youth there and the old Spanish fort, Castillo de San Marcos, is now a National Park site. Really a great place to visit and learn about history and how this state started. There's all kinds of legends and unsolved mysteries about the town and the area. I think it would interest you."

"That does sound interesting, but it'll have to wait. Got another thing that needs looked into and explored and solved first."

Bill nodded and said no more as they drove toward Jacksonville. They should miss morning rush hour traffic but were sure to have to travel through construction zones in the city. Seemed to him, I 95 had always been under construction and reconstruction ever since it was first built. He looked at Roger and saw he was asleep again. *How does he do that? Drink coffee and sleep? At least he'll be alert and in full control of his facilities when they made it to the Greenville area.* Bill knew he needed to be if he wanted this to go as he'd planned and Roger was a very smart and tenacious person when he wanted to be. Thoughts and many different scenarios raced through his mind. He hoped it would work out. It better, or he could be in a world of hurt.

# CHAPTER 7

At the Georgia-Florida line, the boys stopped at the Georgia rest stop, used the facilities again, and switched drivers. Traffic was light for about an hour and a half until they reached the Savannah area. They passed the 8th Air Force Museum honoring the men who fought and some who died in WW II fighting the air war in Europe. Roger made a mental note to visit this place too sometime in the future.

As they approached the bridge over the river into South Carolina, traffic came to a screeching halt. Whatever had happened was just up ahead at the bridge. People were getting out of their cars and running to the bridge.

"Think we can help?" Roger said.

"I don't know. Only one way to find out."

They got out of the truck and hurried forward to the bridge. A big rig was jack-knifed on it, but the most curious thing was a group of people, mainly young women wearing tight shorts bending over the concrete side of the bridge yelling at something or someone below. Roger looked to where they were watching and saw a man wearing soaked clothing standing in thick dark brown water up to his knees in the river. "What's going on?" he asked a bystander.

"Unbelievable," the white-haired man said. "An 18 wheeler hit the back of a port-a-potty truck and pushed it over the side."

"So, that's the driver down in the river?" someone asked.

"Yup, lucky man he's not dead especially to land in a river that shallow," Roger said. "Where's his truck?"

The white-haired man looked at Roger curiously. "You're not from around here, are you?"

"No, what am I missing?"

"Everyone around here knows that river runs deep especially at high tide like it is now. He's standing on the top of the truck cab. It's in the water below him."

"Oh," Roger said. "That sure puts a different perspective on it."

Sirens could be heard and soon the area was crawling with police from several jurisdictions and emergency responders. After looking at the situation, some of the EMTs worked their way down to the river bank and called out to the man. They talked for a minute or so, and as they did, a small boat with a man and a young boy came around a bend in the river. As it approached, they could see the predicament of the wet man and went to his rescue. The truck driver was more than happy to get it the boat. His rescuers took him over to the EMTs on the bank.

As the truck driver got out, the boat tipped, and he fell in the brown water. Two EMTs jumped in and pulled the drenched man to safety on the bank. Once safely on the bank, others had him sit down, and Roger and Bill watched as they checked him out. They seemed satisfied he was okay and shortly afterward, helped him walk up the bank to the interstate highway. Once there, the crowd broke out into spontaneous applause which seemed to embarrass the trucker. He was put in an ambulance that disappeared south going down the shoulder.

With the excitement over, Roger and Bill looked at each other. "Now, what?" a bystander said.

"I guess we wait. Looks like it could take a while," Bill said.

"I think you're right. Looks to me like they'll have to get a wrecker in from the South Carolina side and we're gonna be here a while," the bystander said. "Where you guys going? I'm heading to the little town Travelers Rest north of Greenville."

"We're going the same direction, not quite to Greenville. Simpsonville to be exact," Roger said.

"Simpsonville," the man said. "If you want a great meal, stop in at Poppas and Beer, a super Mexican place that can't be beat."

"Thank you," said Bill.

The boys walked over to the side of the bridge and looked over the side. The top of a blue truck was barely visible. "The water is gonna be running blue downstream from here today," Bill said.

"And crapped up," someone said.

A woman asked, "Wonder how they'll get it out?"

A third person said, "It may be there for some time."

"Maybe, they'll use a big plunger," someone else said. Several people laughed. Numerous heads nodded. With the major excitement over, many motorists walked back to their vehicles. Around 45 minutes later, a large wrecker arrived on the north side of the bridge. It took another 30 for the workers to free the jack-knifed truck and clear the highway. Traffic began flowing northbound, but most of it exited at the first opportunity, the South Carolina rest stop. Bill and Roger were some of the first people to arrive. When they exited the bathrooms, they noted the line outside the ladies room was 10 deep and getting longer. Those needs taken care of, they were back on I 95.

They stopped for lunch at a Shoney's Restaurant, and both had the buffet. Back on the road with Roger driving, Bill soon fell asleep and began to snore. Roger found a country station he liked and sang along with Johnny Cash, Ghost Riders in the Sky, Willie Nelson, and even Jimmy Buffet who was still Wasting Away in Margaritaville. The miles and minutes rolled on as he drove.

Roger stopped at a rest stop on I 26, and a now refreshed Bill took the wheel. He knew the directions to the Miller house in Simpsonville. Traffic through Columbia at rush hour was stop and go, and two hours later, they arrived at their destination. They pulled into the circular drive leading to a brick rancher that had been painted white. A well-manicured lawn with numerous flower beds gave it a crisp and clean appearance.

They parked, walked up the steps to the front door, and knocked. A noise inside told them someone was coming. The front door opened and a black woman stood in front of them. A screen door was between them. Bill said, "Is Mr. Miller in? He should be expecting us."

She questioned, "And you are?"

"I'm Canaveral Flats Chief of Police Bill Kenney, and this is Investigator Roger Pyles."

"Oh," she said. She opened the door. "Won't you come in? My husband has been wondering where you were. You're late. Bathrooms on the right if you need it. Come on down the hallway and make yourselves comfortable in the great room. He's out puttering around in the shed. I'll get him. He's been looking forward to talking with you. He has much to tell that should be of interest to you."

# CHAPTER 8

The woman said, "My name is Cindy. I'll get Clyde. Just take a minute. Help yourself to the coffee in the pot on the counter in the kitchen. There's bottled water in the refrigerator if you prefer."

"Thank you, ma'am," the boys said almost in unison.

The woman went through a doorway into another section of the house, and she had a pronounced limp. As the boys passed where she had gone, they could see the kitchen and two rooms leading off of it, one a living room and one an enclosed porch with lots of windows. Bill went in the bathroom first, and Roger could hear him relieving himself. Soon he could hear water running in a sink as Bill washed his hands. He exited, and Roger went into the bathroom and followed the same routine as Bill had. Roger exited and found his way to the kitchen. Bill had already found the coffee and was sipping on a steaming cup of the black liquid. Roger got a bottle of water and commented, "I wonder if your cousin Tom Kenney up in West Virginia has decided on starting that bottled water business he was talking about?" Roger asked.

"I think he was leaning heavily in that direction. You two sure caused a lot of trouble for me while he was here, and it was mainly you. His wife's still hot about you being a bad influence and nearly getting the two of you arrested on his vacation here. You two cost me a lot of favors with the sheriff's department in keeping you guys out of the pokey. And I'm not going to let you forget it anytime soon."

"Yeah, I do owe you on that. It's good to have friends in low places." Bill gave Roger a dirty look. "Do you really think Sarah would scalp me?"

"I don't think Navajos scalp people, but she may have made an exception in your case." Roger grimaced. Bill continued, "I'd be more worried about her comments to use your foreskin for a nose warmer."

"Glad I'm circumcised," Roger said.

"Not sure that would have stopped her. Be glad she's a thousand miles away and has other matters of more concern at this moment than coming for you. Just the same, I don't think I'd take any trips up north in the near future especially the area around where Tom lives. Not sure if the moccasin express works for her in West Virginia, but the grapevine's very active up there."

"I know about the grapevine. I agree it would be in my best interests not to travel to her neighborhood any time soon."

"You got that right. Something else you need to be aware of, Roger. While this county is growing like wildfire, we have a grapevine here too, especially in the areas where things haven't changed too much."

"Like Canaveral Flats?" Roger asked.

"Yeah, like Canaveral Flats and the surrounding area," Bill said. Most of the growth has been in the south end of the county around Melbourne and Palm Bay where Harris Corporation has moved in, but growth is spreading. One day, the whole county could look like South Florida. Think Miami and Fort Lauderdale area."

"Hope I never see it. Seems urban areas make people crazy."

"Yeah, Miami reminds me of New York City with a tropical spin. I'll stick right where I am and let others handle the urban jungles," Bill said.

"Gloria Hernandez said something similar when I talked to her."

"I'm not surprised. Seems we have a lot of people coming here fleeing from the cities."

"And creating more cities."

"Ironic isn't it?"

"Yeah, but what's you gonna to do?"

Bill sighed, "I know. What's you gonna do?"

At that time, a white man and a black woman came out of the shed and began to walk to the house. She still had a pronounced limp.

Roger looked at Bill. "Is that them?" Bill nodded. "You didn't tell me they were a salt and pepper team."

"I didn't know until she mentioned getting her husband."

"Bet there's some interesting stories about that, this being the old South."

"Yeah, I bet there is. Don't push the issue. We're here on business. If they want to talk about it, leave it to them. You got a problem with that?"

"No, just seems there's been lots of surprises in my life lately."

Bill said, "Yeah, you know the old Chinese curse – 'May you live in interesting times.'"

A little smile came to Roger's face. "Ain't that the truth."

The exterior door opened and the Miller's walked in. Clyde Miller, a man of about 60 with some gray in a full head of hair and a weathered face, spoke, "I see you guys have found some liquid refreshments. Make yourselves at home. We can talk some before dinner. Cindy, you did order from Papas?"

"I sure did just like we talked about." She looked at the boys and said, "I sure hope you fellows like Mexican. Papas is one of our favorite restaurants. We thought you two would probably be hungry and tired after your trip. Y'all welcome to spend the night. We have a guest bedroom we keep handy for guests and family."

Roger looked at Bill. "Sounds good to me. We met a guy on the way up who told us Papas was good. What do you think, Bill?"

Bill said, "It would be greatly appreciated. Mr. Miller, I know you're quite aware of what a cop gets paid."

Mr. Miller said, "I am. That's why I suggested it. You won't be disappointed. There're fresh towels in the bathroom for you to use when you clean up, shower or whatever."

The doorbell rang. Mr. Miller said, "Looks like the restaurant's delivery man's here. I'll get it and Cindy, could you get the table ready?"

"Sure thing, Clyde. The thought of the food is making my mouth water," she said.

Mr. Miller left the kitchen and Cindy went to the cupboards and opened them. "Can we help?" Bill asked.

"Sure thing," she said.

Soon the table was set and the food, burritos, was passed out to eat. After a short prayer, all chowed down on the Mexican food. "Oh, I forgot," Cindy said, "no drinks. Are you guys good with a beer to wash this all down? Coronas?"

"Sounds good to me," Bill said.

"Yeah, me too," Roger said.

She looked at her husband, and he nodded too. Cindy got up, got the beers from the refrigerator, and passed them out. The men all thanked her. She looked at Roger. "Say, had anybody ever told you that you looked and even sound like Sam Elliott?"

"Yup, happens all the time. Wish I had his money," Roger said. "These burritos are pretty good. They were next to none existent where I grew up in West Virginia. The standard fare was meat and taters."

"Seems each area of our country has its own local cuisines. Have you sampled grits or barbeque or greens yet? she asked."

"Barbeque yes, but not the others yet," Roger replied.

"You don't know what you're missing," she said.

"I've eaten some strange things while on digs in foreign countries," Roger said. 'They tasted good, but I wasn't sure I wanted to know what they were. Ever had scrapple, or puddin' or souse Cindy?"

Roger caught a knowing smile slip onto Clyde's face. She said, "No can't say I have. I've heard of souse. Can't be any more interesting than what chitins are made from. What's scrapple anyway?"

Roger said, "Scrapple and puddin' are mainly and normally scrapes left over from the butchered pig with cornmeal added. You fry it and put butter and syrup on it. I like it, but some others find it repulsive. Now souse is even more interesting. It's a form of head cheese. They take scrap meat from the pig mainly from the feet, head, heart, and tongue, pickle it, add salt and sometimes peppers and vinegar, mix it all up, and cook it. It has a very interesting taste."

She smiled, "I'll bet it does. I'd try it. As I said, can't be any worse than anything I've already eaten."

Roger said, "Could I ask you two a personal question?" His eyes shifted from Cindy to Clyde and back. Bill frowned. "It's kind of the elephant in the room, and I've been accused of having curiosity to a fault. You don't have to answer if you don't want to. It is kind of nosey, but this is the South, and you guys are a mixed race couple. There's a story there, and I'd like to hear it if you don't mind."

The couple looked at each other and smiled knowingly. "You wanna start on this Clyde?"

"Sure. No, it's not the first time we've been asked this. It wasn't something we sought out or planned. After my wife died, there were too many bad memories for me back in Florida, and I moved up here. I have a son working for General Electric in Greenville, so I knew a little about the area already. He suggested I come to church with him. Said there were a lot of good people there. Don't know what got into me, but I said yes, and I'm glad I did. The church was a mixture of black and white folks, and they all seemed to get along. I liked that. Most times, Sunday morning is the most segregated time left in America. I met Cindy the first day going in the church. You want to take it from here, Cindy?"

"Okay. I was still recovering from my surgery where I got shot in the leg. I was a cop in Spartanburg. What a time that was. Our force was still integrating, and it wasn't always smooth and being a black female made it even harder. I was out on patrol one night, stopped a car with a light out. I no more than got out of the car when the driver opened fire. I was hit in the leg and went down. I got three shots off at the fleeing car. It was found the next day in a shopping center parking lot. There was blood on the seats. The car had been stolen, but they never did find out who was driving. I nearly bled to death from the wound that went through the tibia. It took a long time to recover, and the doctor said I'd have a limp and need a cane the rest of my life, so my days as a cop were over. I try to do without it around the house, but need it when I'm out and about."

Clyde said, "She thanked me for opening the door. We were a bit late, and the only seats were in the front. They sat us up there. Cindy was next to me, and her singing sent chills through me."

Cindy said, "Growing up, I sang in the choir at an all-black church. Some of us were into Rock and Roll, and we formed a band. Called it the Black Cats. It was some of the best times and worse times in my life. I loved the singing and the crowds, but the booze and drugs and rowdiness wore me down. I knew if I kept on that path, I'd end up dead at a young age. I'd seen so many of my friends come to bad ends. My momma never gave up on me. She was a prayer warrior and not afraid to storm the very gates of Hell. She's the reason I'm still alive, my Momma and Jesus. She died about five years ago. How I miss her. I know she's waiting for me in Heaven." She lowered her eyes, and the boys noted a tear in her eye.

Clyde smiled and put his arm around his wife. He kissed the side of her head. "She gets worked up when she talks about the shooting and her momma." He hugged her. "I was kind of floundering too when I came here. She kind of saved my life too, her and Jesus. We weren't planning on any of this. We weren't trying to make any kind of statement. It just happened, and I'm glad it did. Can you guys understand that?"

Bill looked at Roger, and they both nodded. Bill said, "Yeah, makes sense to me. I'm glad you two are happy together and moving forward."

Roger said, "I'm sorry if I caused you any distress, ma'am."

She wiped away a tear. "No foul, young man. You gave me an opportunity to tell you about us and Jesus. God is good, and sometimes you got to go through some hard times before things work out. It felt like I was being pulled through a knothole. Like the Good Book says, 'There may be pain in the night, but joy comes in the morning. Sorry if I'm getting preachy."

Roger said, "No, thanks for sharing." He paused. "I've been going through some hard times myself and it's always good to hear about people getting through their problems and it all working out."

Bill cleared his throat. "Hey, these burritos are getting cold and the beer warm. Let's eat all up, clean up, and then talk about what we came here for. Sound good?"

All nodded in agreement. They ate quickly and cleaned up just as quickly. They sat down at the table again. Clyde spoke, "I'd like Cindy to sit in on this. She's never heard the whole story, and she may have some new insight and take on it. Is that okay?"

Roger and Bill nodded approval. Clyde said, "Good. I was cruising US 1 just south of Titusville looking for drunks leaving the bars. We'd had a lot of trouble there lately after closing time. I was just done with a safety check on a guy when I got the call. He was stone sober and cool as a cucumber. No problem with him. So, it goes something like this,.."

# CHAPTER 9

Clyde continued, "As I said, I had been looking for drunk drivers when I got the call. It had been a quiet night, a pleasant surprise for me when the call came across the radio. Seemed there had been a big fight at a bar party on the north end of town and just about all of the Titusville cops on duty were up there trying to restore order and clean up the mess. There had been a couple of stabbings or more, and at least one person had been shot. As you well know, all the police forces in the county have a mutual assistance agreement. Brevard County Deputies assist the city cops when needed, and vice versa and I was the closest unit.

"I pulled into the parking lot at the Canaveral Diner a little after 4 o'clock. The report I got from the 911 people was of a stabbing with injuries. I was met at the door by the owner who I knew. He was a train wreck with tears flowing down his face, and he was visibly shaking. His eyes said it all. I knew it was bad.

"He told me she was on the floor in the kitchen and sat down in a booth. He asked if I had a cigarette and I said no. He said he quit years ago, but could sure use one now. I opened the swinging door into the kitchen and was not prepared for what I saw, and I've seen a lot. She was laying there nude face up spread eagle with multiple stab wounds in her body, my guess was at least twenty.

"There were two things that struck me as odd. One, with all the stab wounds, I expected blood splattered everywhere. It was not so. And two, her clothing was neatly folded in a pile nearby. Blood ran from under her body to a nearby floor drain. A bloody butcher knife lay on the counter, and it had a broken off point. I thought she may have been raped. She was definitely dead. I secured the area and called in a quick report. It was at that time Chief of Police of Canaveral Flats Bill Kenney showed up. He was in street clothes. Bill, I think we need your input now."

"Okay, I can give some information. I was in the area and had my radio on. I heard the call and decided to help. Seemed there weren't too many cops available because of the big fight. The owner let me in and pointed to the kitchen. He said another cop was already there. I opened the door and found Clyde, Officer Miller, in the kitchen, and there was crime tape around the area. He did not recognize me at first and asked, quote, "What the hell are you doing here and who the bleep are you?' I told him, and he remembered me. He said he hadn't expected me here and out of uniform, too. Remember that?"

Clyde said, "I do. The bad old days. My language has changed and improved over the years."

Cindy cut in. "What were you doing there at that place at that hour of the morning and in street clothes?"

Bill replied, "As I said, I'd been in the area and was on my way home when I heard the call."

"What had you been doing?" Cindy asked.

"I'm not at liberty to say," Bill said.

Cindy shot her husband a questioning look, but Clyde let it pass.

Bill said, "I know what you're thinking, and I don't blame you. And FYI, it gets more complicated for me. The dead woman was my former girlfriend, and our recent breakup had been high volume. Apparently, we were not on the same page when it came to seeing other people. In no uncertain terms, she let me know she thought I'd betrayed her by being with other women and she was mad as hell about it.

"She was yelling and tried to hit me several times, but I deflected the blows. She threw a glass ashtray at me. Glad I had fast reflexes and ducked, but it nearly hit a county Deputy who showed up at the time. He saw who'd thrown it and took charge. He kept us apart and sorted things out. She said she never wanted to see me again and I could rot in hell for all she cared. The Deputy asked if I wanted to press charges as he could see the marks on my arms and knew she had winged the ashtray at me. I said no. I wasn't interested in seeing charges were filed. By then, things were calming down. The Deputy asked us what we wanted. She said she wanted me to get the bleeping bleep out and never come back. I told him I'd do that and left. I never saw her again until that night in the restaurant kitchen."

"Why won't you tell us where you were earlier?" Cindy inquired. "An alibi would come in real handy right now. It seems you had a motive."

Bill said, "An alibi would be real handy. That is correct, but I have my reasons for my silence. Jumping ahead, the inquiry did list me as one of the suspects, but lack of evidence soon turned this into a cold case and here we are today. Roger helped various police departments solving crimes when he lived up north. He had his reasons for coming to Florida. I'll let him give them if needed. He's a forensics expert and helped solve a murder in our little town recently. A body was found buried in a peat bog swamp during a housing development construction. I deputized him, and he has agreed to help on this cold case."

"I hope this one doesn't almost get me killed like the last one did," Roger said. "I can still see that green laser light from that sniper's gun. If it hadn't been for a rescue dog I'd recently got at the pound who alerted me, I wouldn't be alive today."

"So a rescued dog rescued you?" Clyde said.

"She did as the Shaman said she would, but that's another story," Roger said.

Clyde and Cindy looked at Roger and then to Bill when Roger said no more.

Bill said, "It's a long story best told another time. It's got nothing to do with our cold case, and I'd like to get this over. It's been a long ride here, and I'd like to get some shuteye soon if that's okay. Clyde, could you finish this off for now? If we have any more questions or you remember anything additional, we can discuss it before we leave town tomorrow morning."

"We'd like you guys to stay the night. We have a king size bed in the guest room. There's only one bed. If you don't mind sharing a bed, we have one available," Cindy said.

"Sounds good to me," Bill said. "What about you, Roger? You game with that?"

Roger looked at Bill sideways and said, "Bill, you certainly aren't my first choice for a bedmate. Last time I slept with another person was my late wife. I bet you snore and have stinking feet."

"I'll shower up and take care of the feet, but I do snore some, I'm told," Bill said.

Roger said, "It's against my better judgment on having Bill for a bedmate, but I'm tired too, and the price is right." He stopped. "What more do you have to add, Clyde?"

"Not sure I have much more. The forensics guy showed up, took lots of pictures, dusted for fingerprints, took the bloody knife, took statements, checked us for blood splatter, found none, and looked for anything else out of place. Clues are always left, but this one gave us only a few, and those all lead to dead ends. If I remember correctly, the ex-husband was another suspect, but he had an alibi of some sort. The other possibility considered was an unknown suspect who took advantage of the situation and went on a bloody frenzy."

"Thanks, Clyde," Bill said, "And the money that was in a flimsy locked box in the back was not taken. Robbery didn't seem to be the original motive."

"That is interesting," Cindy said. "Think it's time to turn in. I'd like to sleep on this and see what if anything comes from the little gray cells as Poirot likes to say."

Roger said, "Ah, I see you're a fan of Agatha Christie."

"I am," Cindy said. "I really loved the story, 'And Then There Were None,' even if the stories' title has been changed several times."

"I didn't know that," Roger said. "'Murder on the Orient Express' is my favorite." He paused and yawned. "It's time. We'll get our stuff from the vehicle, clean up, and see you in the morning."

"Sounds like a plan," Cindy said. "If you need anything just holler. Good night."

Good nights were exchanged, and the boys retrieved their suitcases from outside. Bill told Roger to use the bathroom first, and he did. A quick shower and he stripped off to his undershorts and slipped into bed. Bill took a quick shower and entered the bedroom. He stripped off all of his clothing, tossed them carelessly on the floor, and crawled into bed under the sheet.

Roger looked at Bill. "You never told me you slept in the nude."

Bill said, "It's not something I usually shout to the world. You got a problem with that?"

Roger gave a harrumphing sound. "I've slept with a lot of naked women, but no, I've never slept with a naked man."

"First time for everything. You could sleep on the floor if

it bothers you."

"You sleep on the floor with your clothes you threw everywhere. Is your place in Canaveral Flats as messy as you made this place?"

"No, it's more so."

"Pig."

"I've been called that before, sometimes on the job."

The two men said nothing for a moment. Roger asked, "You're not going to kiss me, are you?"

"Sorry, not even if you beg me. You're not my type."

"Bill, you're disgusting."

"And naked."

"Naked and disgusting."

Bill said, "Now we have that revelation, will you shut up, and we can get some sleep?"

"And no kissing."

"No kissing, not even if you beg. Satisfied?"

"I'd be more satisfied if you sleep on the floor."

"Ain't gonna happen. You could sleep on the floor."

Roger said, "Oh, never mind. If you touch me, I'm not responsible for what happens."

"Okay. Happy now?"

"Not really."

"You'll get over it."

"I'm still not gonna like it. If word of this gets out..."

"It won't. That's funny coming from the guy whose dog liked to ruined my truck."

Roger snickered, "Now that was funny. So they're still calling you Stinky from where she vomited and crapped in it?"

"Not funny. Not funny at all."

Roger laughed. "Good night, Bill. Sleep tight. Lots of skin exposed for the bugs to bite." Roger thought he heard a growl.

"Good night, Roger."

Roger whispered, "Good night, Stinky."

"I heard that. You make me want to hurt someone very close to me."

With a lilt in his voice, Roger said, "Good Night, Bill."

"Good night."

It was only a short time before the two tired men were sound asleep and Bill was snoring loudly, but Roger made it a duo. In another room on the other side of the house, another couple was talking in their bed.

"Well, what did you think, Cindy?"

"It felt like old times, talking shop with a bunch of cops. I hope we were of some help in bringing this case to a conclusion. Not sure we were."

"Cold cases can be hard to crack. Sometimes, new eyes will see something that was missed. Sometimes just stirring the pot will get the killer's attention and he'll do something that will expose him. Sometimes he won't even know it till it's too late."

"Yeah, and sometimes stirring the pot will put the lives of the detectives at risk when they get close to the truth whether they realize it at the time or not."

"True," Clyde said. "What do you think of those two?"

"They seem like good men. The woman in me thinks Roger has seen great pain in his life, but he's trying to hide it from us. He seems dedicated and determined to finding out what happened. Now, ole Bill, on the other hand, is another story. Something about his story is a few bricks short of a load. Is he here to help or is he trying to sidetrack the investigation, or maybe even led it astray? His showing up where he did that night raises many questions. It would be so easy for him to clear himself if he provided an alibi, but something seems to be holding him back and I can't imagine what it could be that would be that important to keep quiet."

"Cindy, that's about my take on it, too."

"Any other thoughts on it before I turn out the light?"

"No."

She turned out the light, and as the room darkened, Cindy crawled on top of Clyde. "Hmm," Clyde said. "What's this all about?"

Clyde could hear the cooing in her voice. "Why honey, you've just been blacktopped."

"Oh," he said pleasantly. "Guess that means I'm about to be road?"

"It does. You just stay in the center lane and put the pedal to the metal. Don't stop till we meet our destination."

Clyde said, "I feel like a railroad crossing barrier, and the train has just roared through."

"I can tell. Your bar has just risen to the upright position. Ding, ding, ding."

They kissed. Nothing more needed to be said. The lights were all green and would stay locked in that position till the sweet ride was over.

◆ ◆ ◆

Roger woke the next morning to the smell of coffee and bacon. Bill was still sleeping and snoring. Roger slip out of bed, dressed in the dim light, found his way to the bathroom, and relieved his full bladder. He washed his hands and headed toward the kitchen. Clyde sipped on a cup of coffee as he read the morning newspaper. Cindy was fixing breakfast. She said, "I thought I heard someone. Where's your friend, Bill?"

"Still sleeping."

Clyde said, "Care for coffee, Roger?"

"Sure. Sounds great."

"How do you like it?"

Roger said, "I like mine hot and black."

Cindy laughed but tried to swallow it. Clyde nearly choked as he was sipping the coffee

"Did I say something funny?" a puzzled Roger asked. "Oh," he said as he saw why his choice of words had created such a reaction.

Clyde got Roger a cup. "Here you go, hot and black, like we like it."

Roger cleared his throat before taking a sip. "This hits the spot. You didn't have to fix us breakfast."

"I insist," Cindy said. "Nothing like Southern Hospitality and you are in the South even if you had to come north to be in the South."

"Roger said, "Yeah, it is kind of funny how you have to drive north to find an area with a majority of southern accents. Not too many crackers left in central Florida anymore as the place grows like a well-fertilized weed after an all-day rain."

"Got a question for you, Roger, before Bill gets up. Do you think he did it?" Clyde asked.

"I'm not sure. I'm not sure if he's helping or leading me astray like a man leads a bull with a ring in his nose around. I have my doubts, but I haven't ruled him out. Trying to keep an open mind and not let our friendship get in the way. I want this solved one way or the other."

Cindy looked at Roger curiously. He noticed her look. "What?" he said.

"Has anyone ever told you that you like Sam Elliott?" she said."

He smiled. "Yeah, happens all the time," he drawled in his best Sam Elliott imitation. "Remember? You asked me last night."

"So I did. Sorry, I forgot," she said.

"You do favor him," Clyde said. "You even sound like him."

The trio made more small talk for about fifteen minutes. Bill appeared at the kitchen doorway. His hair was in his eyes. "I smell coffee."

"Cup'll be waiting for you," Clyde said.

Bill smiled, "Bathroom first. Got to get rid of some fluid before I add more." He disappeared.

Clyde laughed, "I know about getting old and having to go all the time."

Cindy said, "We hit every rest area when we travel, either to go or stretch or both."

"Yup, sounds about like me and Bill," Roger said.

When Bill came back, breakfast was waiting for him. They ate and chatted after a short grace said by Cindy. No one really had anything of significance to add to the information already discussed the day before. All exchanged phone numbers and agreed to contact each other if needed. Roger and Bill thanked them for their hospitality and kindness. As they drove off, Cindy said to Clyde, "Do you think they will find an answer?"

"I do, and it may be a surprise."

"Don't be too sure on that Clyde. I have this feeling if anyone can crack this case, it will be Roger."

Clyde nodded, "On that, we agree."

# CHAPTER 10

The boys had no more than reached the Interstate on the way home when Bill said to Roger, "You told me how you met your wife and ended up married to her when we talked before, but you never told me much about her. Care to share anything on this long ride home?"

Roger looked at Bill and said, "Okay, but I've got some questions for you about your involvement with this cold case. Care to give me some candid answers?"

"Sure. Go ahead and tell me about your late wife and then I'll answer any questions you have. Sound good?"

"It does. Let me tell you about Kay. You know she was pregnant when we got hitched. Fortunately for us, the morning sickness stopped shortly before our wedding. My troubles at the university were just getting started, so I had little difficulty getting time off for a honeymoon. They found a sub for Kay while we were gone.

"We found some reasonably priced tickets on Southwest Airlines, some kind of a special sale they were having. Guess they had some seats they needed to fill. Anyway, we got round trip tickets to Denver, rented a car, and took off to see the mountains and the West. Kay hadn't traveled much and had listened with envy when I told her of my travels on work detail."

"Yeah, I thought you'd been around the pike a few times," Bill said.

"I have and hope to be able to do more of that in the

future. Kay was a great traveling companion and it being our honeymoon, we rocked many a bed during our trip."

Bill snickered at that and Roger said, "We may have got the cart before the horse when we started out, but once we were married, it was all good in her mind, and she was a great wife and lover. And no, I won't go into the intimate details. Besides, your imagination is probably better than the truth."

"True, Roger. I'm glad you're withholding the details. I always thought what happened in a bedroom between a husband and wife was kinda sacred and personal and not something to be shared with others. Some of my standards may be low, but I do have a few."

"Agreed, ain't none of your business. I respect Kay and her memory too much to go blabbing about matters such as that. Anyway, we planned on a loop starting and ending in Denver. We weren't sure if we wanted a big circle or a little loop with the southernmost point being Santa Fe, New Mexico. It all depended on the weather.

"Well, we saw some friends of mine in Denver, drove to Colorado Springs, and got snowed on. The next day, the weather broke, and there wasn't a cloud in the sky. We decided to see how far we could make it up the road to Pike's Peak. Made it to 12,000 feet before the road was closed because of the new snowfall. What a view. It sure didn't look like our home in the Appalachians."

"Or Florida," Bill said.

"Or Florida. It was absolutely beautiful, but the altitude gave us both headaches. After seeing the Garden of the Gods, we took some mountain backroads, went through several old mining towns, and then down a dirt road that used to be a narrow gauge railroad years ago. What a ride that was down the narrow twists and turns in the 20-mile long canyon, maybe longer. We had a mountain on one side and nothing on the other in places.

Saw all kinds of critters, a mother bear with her cub, a bighorn ram, and a whole bunch of elk and mule deer."

"No alligators?" Bill asked.

"No alligators, but there was a place near the Great Sand Dunes National Park that advertised Colorado gators."

"Really?"

"Yeah, it started as a fish farm in a hot spring, and the owner got the idea of having gators to clean up the fish guts, and he then expanded it into a reptile farm, but the gators were the main draw, though we did not stop. After overnighting in Canyon City, we drove to Raton, NM and drove up the Capulin Volcano National Monument. It was a great view, but not a place I'd want to be in during a lightning storm, it being mainly rock with lots of iron in it."

"Sounds like it would have made a good lightning rod," Bill said.

"That was my thoughts, too. There was a drought going on, so rain wasn't a concern. We stopped at the NRA Center nearby and did some shooting. Kay turned about to be quite a good shot. She surprised me."

"Women will do that."

"Yeah, that Kay was full of surprises. We stayed in Santa Fe two nights at a place on old Route 66 called the Silver Saddle Motel. The rooms all had western themes. We got the Clint Eastwood room the first night and had to move to another room the second. That one was about Roy Rogers, the King of the Cowboys."

"Interesting."

"Old Roy was a smart guy for a country boy from Ohio," Roger said.

"Never make the mistake of underestimating a country

boy. So the king of the cowboys was from back east?'

"He was. Leonard Slye was his real name. The Hollywood producers came up with his stage name. They wanted something similar to Will Rogers who was really popular at that time. Old Roy was a sharp fellow. He got the complete rights to the name. He even allowed a roast beef restaurant to use it, of course for a fee. Got a Roy Roger's Roast Beef in Cumberland, Maryland. Darn good food, too."

"That does sound like a wise man," Bill said.

"He just recently retired after a long and successful career. Age will do that to you."

"It will. I think he's enjoying his time out to pasture.

"So much for Roy. We went to a huge caldera, the third largest in the US and the next day drove over to Durango past Georgia O'Keeffe country. Beautiful but stark area. We rode the Durango to Silverton Narrow Gauge Railroad on Mothers Day. Incredible scenery and she got a flower. Oh, and a bunch of hippies down by the Animas River mooned us on the way back."

Bill rolled his eyes. "What would we do without hippies?"

Roger laughed. "I told Kay I was going to moon them back, but a sharp elbow jab in my ribs changed my mind."

"I'll bet it did," Bill said.

"We had a meal in the historic Strater Hotel in Durango where Louis L'Amour wrote many of his books. The old bar area, most of which is now a restaurant, still has holes in the tin ceiling from gunshots. A bunch of card games turned deadly and ended fast the hard way years ago."

"Sounds like you guys had some fun."

"We did. The Million Dollar Highway with its twists, turns, switchbacks, and no guard rails was our next adventure."

"No guard rails on a mountain road?" Bill said.

"Nope. Some years, they get 300 inches or more of snow and guard rails would make pushing that much snow off the road impossible, so, no guard rails. We make it to Grand Junction, saw Colorado National Monument with its many colored rock formations, swam in a hot spring in Glenwood Springs, and had a beautiful drive to Leadville which is over 10,000 feet about sea level."

Bill said, "What a change. About 25 feet here in Canaveral Flats."

"I joined the two-mile-high club there."

Bill rolled his eyes. "Honeymooners."

Roger smiled. "The trip back to Denver was beautiful, and we flew back home. Oh, by the way, the airport sits on the edge of the Great Plains, and the uneven heating of the air can make for a bumpy ride leaving. Someone in the front lost their lunch."

"I'll remember that if I go to Denver," Bill said.

"Just depends on the time of day and weather conditions. You never know." Roger paused. "Okay, I've been running my mouth for some time. How about you start telling me about your relationship to the murdered woman?"

"Okay, but you ain't gonna believe this."

"Try me. I'm all ears."

# CHAPTER 11

"Well, as you know every state's laws have some quirks and the great state of Florida is no exception," Bill said.

"I'm aware of that. And some make little or no sense at all," Roger said.

"It was one of those quirks that led me to meet Missy McCoy Odom. The laws in our state leave public and private nudity up to the county or municipality."

"That explains all the crazy laws governing strip joints and other places that vary from county to county and city to city."

"We're on the same track, Roger. In Brevard and Volusia County, we have the federal Canaveral National Seashore, a beautiful area with no bars, or condos, or hotels, just natural sand beaches. There are no federal laws on nudity so for years the remote north end of the national seashore has been a place where nudists come to sun their buns and have for decades. There's usually not too much trouble with them, and they spend a bunch of money."

"Not on swimsuits."

"Well, yes, they do. They need them till they get away from the general public. They park at the last lots and then walk north a good way to separate themselves from the clothed public beachgoers. Some time ago, the county passed an ordinance banning nudity on all beaches in the county. Our local sheriff had never sent his people up there before. He left the feds to take care of any problems, but the feds weren't interested in enforcing the county's statute, so it was up to him to take care of it. To keep the county commissioners and concerned public off his back, about once or twice a year, he would send someone up there to see the beachgoers complied with the regulation."

"Bill, this is all very interesting, but what's it got to do with Missy?"

"Have patience, young friend. I listened to your yarn about you and your wife, and now you can listen to mine."

"All right. Get to the point, Bill."

"I was before I was so rudely interrupted."

Roger gave him a dirty look and Bill continued. "The sheriff couldn't find anyone for this fool's errand, and I took the job."

"Fool's errand? I'd think most of the deputies would jump at the chance to get their eyes full."

"You would think that, but word had gotten out that it was mainly seasoned citizens frequenting the area on the days the sheriff picked for selective enforcement."

"Seasoned citizens?" Roger said. "You mean like seniors, 65 and above retired people?"

"You got it, old boy. Not the most pleasant specimens to lay eyes on."

"Bill, I'll agree with that. So why did you take it?"

"What else? The money. I sometimes moonlight for extra money, usually as a security guard over at Kennedy Space Center or Cape Canaveral just like my dad did, but other places too. I'd already passed the federal background check, so I was a shoo-in."

"Okay. So far, so good. Continue."

"I got the job and drove to the end of the road at

Playalinda Beach. Took me a while to find a parking spot as the lot was full. Finally, a spot opened up as an elder couple was leaving. I took it, parked, and started up the beach. I walked a quarter mile before I ran into the first naked people. I told them about the regulation, and they covered up. I repeated this as I walked up the beach and the people complied, some grudgingly, but they complied, and that was that. As I said, most were seniors. I could tell some were regulars by the leathery skin and some not. The latter either were putting copious amounts of sunscreen on or were quite red like boiled lobsters."

"Bet that was gonna hurt the next day," Roger said.

"Yup. A carpenter friend who used to live in the Flats once told me how he was working down Miami way and on the weekend went to a nudie beach down there. I did some construction work also before becoming a cop. Alcohol flowed freely with the group he was with. He said he played nude volleyball and really got his eyes full that day, but there was a downside."

"I think I know where you're going."

Bill nodded, "Yeah, he got an allover sunburn. He was in no pain while under the influence, but the next day or two was horrible. No amount of aloe could stop the pain, and the worst of it was the pain on his hips from where he wore his tool belt. He said he was never gonna do that again."

"Painful lessons can be great learning experiences. They can leave a lasting impression that you remember for a long, long time," Roger said.

"It definitely left an impression on my carpenter friend. Now let's see. Where was I? Oh, yeah, getting people to obey the law by covering up. I walked on down the beach, and there was this shapely thing lying on a towel face down. I told she needed to cover up and everything would be fine. She rolled over, looked up at me, stood up on her tiptoes, and we looked at each other through our sunglasses. Let me tell you, she was built like a brick house. She stood about 5 foot 5 inches, had the breasts ever woman wished for, and all the other parts looked great too. I guessed her measurements were about 37-24-36. She looked a lot like Janet Leigh in the Alfred Hitchcock Psycho movie."

"So Bill, you're telling me she was stacked."

"Yup and this was how I met Missy McCoy Odom. She gave me a hard time at first, but she soon saw it was in her best interest to put on her suit. I never got her name that day. I could have arrested her and hauled her in just like I found her. I told her I would too. I had to do that one time when I found a young guy all drunked up skinny dippin' in a motel pool. He begged for some clothes, but I took him to booking just like that. As I left him there, I hear him say, 'I ain't never gonna do that again.'"

"Yup," Roger laughed. "You remember those painful lessons."

"I saw him sometime later. He was sober this time and not too mad at me. And again, he said he was never gonna do that again, so we parted on good terms."

"Could we get back to Missy?"

"Sure Roger. I went on down the beach doing what I was sent out there to do. After about a mile walk, I turned around and headed back to my vehicle. People were still covered up, but as I passed, they went back to their birthday suits. I'd done what I'd been sent out there to do and reported that to the sheriff and all was well.

"A week later, I pulled over a speeder on US 1. It was a young woman who said she was late for her job at a nearby diner in Titusville. I checked her driver's license, insurance, and registration. All was in order. I decided to write her a warning, and it was at that time, she asked if I didn't recognize her. I said no, and she reminded me of our encounter on the beach. I took a good look at her and said, 'I didn't recognize you with your clothes on.' She laughed, thanked me for letting her off easy, and told me to stop in at the diner. I did later, and before long she was one of my girlfriends."

"One of your girlfriends?" Roger asked.

"Yeah, we'd been together for some time, but our ideas on the relationship were not in sync. She thought it was to be exclusively me and her. When she found out I had other lady friends I was spending the night with, she went ballistic. I never kept it from her, but never spoke about it either. Anyway, it wasn't pretty, and she told me in no uncertain terms she never wanted to see me again. Her pet name for me was 'Love.' Boy, oh boy, did she put a snarl on that term when she stormed off."

"Bill, that doesn't sound good. You could sure help yourself by providing an alibi."

"Roger, I have my reasons, and when this is over, you'll understand."

They rode on in silence for a few minutes. Roger spoke, "So what more could you tell me about her and anything she may have told you about her relationship with her ex-husband."

"As I said, she had a body that other women envied and wished they had and she was not afraid to show it. She gave me a key to her apartment and often when I'd let myself in, I find her nude watching the TV."

"What shows did she like?" Roger questioned.

"Oh, I Love Lucy, Jackie Gleeson, Andy Griffith, and the like. Why do you ask?"

"Just curious, may be important, maybe not."

"Her showing her body off was the biggest problem with her ex. It was okay before they got married, but afterward, he wanted all that to be exclusively for him. She thought different. She continued going out to the nudie beach and even was in a couple of those boob movies teenage boys like," Bill said.

"Boob movies?"

"Yeah, lots of pretty girls running around naked with lots of boob shots and little to no plot in the movie. You know, the kind that appeals to horny teenage boys. She said it paid well, even the one where she was only a pair of breasts framed in a window. She was listed in the credits as Anonymous Torso. Missy believed everyone would know it was her. She said, 'Breasts and nipples are like fingerprints. No two are alike.'"

"Yeah, I know the type of movie. Cheap to make and a good return on the dollar for the producer," Roger said.

"Yup. Her husband was getting very jealous and possessive. She said she had enough and walked out. I think she may have gotten a restraining order again him for all the good they do."

"Another unhappy ending for her."

"Yup, and then she got killed," Bill said.

"And that's where I come in."

"Yup. Roger, if anyone can find out who done it, it will be you."

Roger nodded. "Say, are you good? I'd like to get some shut eye. I may have some more questions when I wake up. You good with that?"

Sure, you get a nap, ask your questions, and then you drive, and I nap. Sound like a plan?"

"It does." Roger pulled his hat down over his eyes and was soon snoring.

Bill looked at Roger and wondered about the gears turning in his sleeping mind. Bill knew how people often get answers after sleeping on it, and he wondered about Roger. *Hope all his gears are properly synchronized. There's a lot riding on them being so.*

◆ ◆ ◆

"Where are we? How long have I been asleep?" Roger asked.

"Sleepyhead, you've been sawing logs for about 45 minutes, and we're just outside of Columbia. Need a pit stop?"

"Soon, but I can wait a little. I think we hit every one so far coming and going."

Bill said, "We may have missed one, maybe two. There's a rest stop on the south side of Columbia about 20 miles or less out. Can you wait that long?"

"Should be no problem. If it is, I can always relieve myself on the floor of your truck."

Bill growled, "Like your dog, K9, did? I told you, I'm still getting a hard time from some of the cops in Brevard County. I'm getting' tired of hearing it. Don't push your luck, ole buddy. It's getting really old."

"Okay, still sore about that are we?" Roger said.

"Yup, it wouldn't be so funny if the shoe was on the other foot."

"True, but it's not," and then Roger gave his best Sam Elliott snicker.

"If we weren't friends, I might abandon you at the rest stop, ole buddy."

"Okay, I'll behave," and he snickered again, but just enough for Bill to notice.

"Ain't funny," Bill snorted.

The two men said nothing for a good minute. Bill asked, "Did you think of any good questions you wanted to ask?"

"None for you yet, but I think I need to talk with some people when we get back home. Missy's ex would be a good one along with the coroner. I'm sure I'll think of others. The more I learn, the better I understand this case."

"Well, I have a question for you," Bill said.

"Shoot."

"What was your most difficult case?"

Roger grunted. "Most difficult case? Hard to say. There's been several. One of the hardest was telling some of the local cops back home their open and shut slam dunk case against a guy was more full of holes than a Swiss cheese. They weren't happy, and I think they're still sore about it. I saved an innocent man from a murder trial, maybe even execution."

"Go on, Roger. This sound interesting."

"This guy was as poor as a church mouse. He'd recently gotten married. He and his new wife lived in an efficiency apartment the size of a shoe box. Their place had a Murphy bed. When you pulled it down, you couldn't open the front door without lifting up the bed. There was no way to get in without raising it. The young man woke up one morning and found his new wife on the floor where she had fallen out of their bed. He picked her up, found she was cold to the touch, but still tried to give her artificial respiration. He pulled her tongue forward, but trying to revive her didn't work.

"He concluded she was dead and put her on the couch, lifted the bed, and went for help. The coroner discovered she died of suffocation, noted bruise marks on her neck, and determined she had been murdered. I was asked to look into it, and a few simple questions saved the man. The dead woman's sister told me she had epilepsy, something she hadn't revealed to her new husband. The sister had once saved her from choking to death on her tongue during a seizure. And the bruises? The dead woman had a friend who thought he was a chiropractor and practiced on her. He did the bruising while cracking her neck. Everyone all saw it as a clear-cut case of murder. Everyone but me."

"Very interesting. Anything else you would like to tell me before we stop?" Bill said.

"Yeah, the important thing in solving crimes, especially murder, is getting inside peoples' heads. People kill people for some reason – hate, love, greed, or revenge. Sometimes they're high on dope or crazy. A good detective must get inside them to find the whos, the whats, and the whys."

"Roger, from all my years in law enforcement, I know that can be a frightening place." He paused. "Anything else you would like to add?"

"Yeah, treat others like you'd like to be treated when they merit such treatment. I got that from my wife who got it from the Bible. And one last word that's even simpler when solving a crime. Work hard and use common sense."

Bill nodded, "Think you're onto something. Couldn't have said it better myself. If anyone can find Missy's killer, it'll be you."

Roger gave Bill a look that shouted, Even if it's you.

Bill read Roger's look and smiled slightly.

Bill said, "Looks like we're here. We'll pit stop and then you drive, Roger."

"Okay, I thought of a few questions. Are you up for them before you take your little nap while I'm driving?"

"Yeah, I think so."

"I got some good ones for you."

Bill nodded. "I'll bet you do."

# CHAPTER 12

The boys were lucky they were boys. There was a line out the door for the ladies room as so often happens. They took care of their business. They noted as they left, the line for the ladies room didn't seem to be moving and had gotten longer. Soon they were back on Interstate 26 heading south.

Bill looked over from the passenger's seat at Roger and asked, "So you got some questions? Let's hear 'em before my date with the Sandman starts."

"Okay," Roger said. "What's your impression of Agent Hernandez?"

"Overall, good. One tough cookie who's trying to do her job and do it well. Got a soft streak like most good cops, but she tries to cover it up. Thinks she needs to fit in and be one of the boys."

"You seem to know a lot about her. Was she one of your lovers, Bill?"

Bill grinned. "That's privileged information. No comment."

This brought a smile to Roger's face.

Bill began again. "I can see why she left Miami. That place is crazy. You should be glad you live up here and not there."

"Tell me more," Roger said.

"Okay and I'll try not to embellish it. It's weird enough without doing so. There's a lot of crime, a whole lot. I saw this bumper sticker recently. It said, '**Please come back to Miami**! We weren't shooting at **You**.'"

"I thought you said you weren't going to embellish it, Bill."

"I'm not. I'm just getting started. Think *Miami Vice* and *Scarface*. In truth, only a small percentage are violent criminals, the bulk of which are elected officials. Most are hardworking people trying to raise their kids well, ready to lay down covering fire when they go outside to pick up their newspapers."

"You're embellishing that, aren't you?" Roger asked.

"Just a little. I'll stick to the truth. Some Norwegian tourists landed at Miami International Airport. On the courtesy bus to their hotel, the bus was boarded by two men who diverted it and robbed them at gunpoint. At another hotel, a German who spent the night complained to the staff as he checked out that the room had a bad smell. They sent a maid to check it out, and she found a corpse under the bed and not a fresh one," Bill said.

"I thought you said you were sticking to the truth."

"I am. If I'm lyin', I'm dyin'. It's not Disney World. They've had shootouts at baby showers and wakes. And the traffic, the young guys drive like maniacs, like they stole the cars and they probably did. Why, then there's the seniors who's awareness of their surroundings is about the same as a ham salad sandwich without relish. They found a confused old guy lost and driving in of all places, the Miami Airport."

"What's so odd about that?" Roger said.

"He was on Runway 9, not I 95."

"That is weird."

Bill said, "At least he had insurance and two handguns with him. Oh, I just remembered another one. They have a free public transportation people mover they call the Metromover. One evening at rush hour, two guys got on carrying a live, six-foot-long nurse shark. They caught it in the bay and were taking it downtown to try and sell it. Only in Miami. When the wholesaler downtown wouldn't buy the shark now dead, they dumped it in the street where it laid for two days."

Roger laughed, "Guess public transportation did not agree with it."

Bill said, "Miami City Highway Maintenance picked it up after someone finally complained."

"So it was just another average day in Miami? Someone would have reported it in a heartbeat in Pittsburgh."

Bill said, "Welcome to Miami. The local paper, The Herald, treated it as a feel-good story for against all the odds, it wasn't a human body."

"At least, it didn't bite anyone."

"I've heard they do animal sacrifice at the hospitals as a medical procedure even though it was discredited a hundred years ago. And the critters down there are far worse than here. The grasshoppers are the size of sparrows. There's poison toads, lizards the size of small dogs, and all kinds of dangerous exotic animals like pythons and New Yorkers."

"Really, Bill?"

"Really, the pythons have taken over the Everglades, a muck-filled swamp where the native grass has saw blades that'll cut you to pieces. Those snakes have eaten about everything else. And don't get me off on the New Yorkers."

"What about them?"

"Roger, they've been coming for years. The upstaters aren't so bad, almost normal, but those from the city when they get there, all they do is bitch about it's so much better up north. They won't root for the local teams. They stick with the Jets, Knicks, Mets, and Yankees. They loudly proclaim the New York restaurants were better, stores nicer, people smarter, and that there's never been a shark on public transportation, etc. I don't know why they left their little paradise."

Roger laughed, "And let me guess, they won't leave their new home now."

"Nope, not on your life. I guess the really worst thing is they didn't leave their stinkin' thinkin' up there. They're now using the same thinkin' to turn Florida into the place they wouldn't go back to. Not even Tim Dorsey could make up this stuff."

"Who? Can't say I've heard of him?"

"Well, Roger. I'm surprised. A man of your stature not knowing Tim Dorsey?"

"Can't say I do. How do you know him?"

"Well, I wrote him a ticket."

"What? You wrote him a ticket?" Roger said.

"Yeah," he sighed. "I got to admit I didn't know who he was till I pulled him over for speeding on US 1. People treat that road like they're on the interstate. I pulled this big white Lincoln over. The car was full of boxes and duffle bags. I wondered if he might be a drug runner."

Roger said, "Yeah, he could have been dangerous."

"Dangerous? He was dangerous. We got to talking, and he had me laughing so hard, I thought I was gonna die. I almost cried. Well, his papers were in order, and he was on his way to a book signing at the Titusville Public Library. He invited me. I went, and everyone there had a good time even though he brought the roof down."

"How'd he do that?" Roger asked.

Ole Tim was getting all animated talking about two characters in his book, Serge and Coleman. I think I might have met the guys he patterned the men after when I worked as a carpenter some years ago. Tim was waving his hands around like a traveling hellfire and brimstone country preacher, and he knocked his coffee cup off the podium. It went flying and shattered when it hit the floor. Coffee and pieces of the ceramic cup went everywhere. He was embarrassed, but recovered quickly as the library staff cleaned up the mess. The library has since put up signs stating no food or drinks are allowed in the library."

"That must have been exciting."

Bill said, "It was, but it also made him more human. Some people get the big head when they've written several books that sold millions."

Roger laughed. "Looked like ole Tim sure did a good job of making himself humble that day."

"He did. I bought one of his books. He made me pay full price even though I let him off with a warning."

"Sounds like an author. Pretty tight with his money."

"They are. Trust me. I know first-hand," Bill said

Roger said, "I believe you. Say, you've been talking a lot. Ask me something."

"Okay." Bill rubbed his chin as he thought. "Tell me something funny about yourself and then something serious."

A big smile came to Roger's face. "As you know, I've got a soft spot in my heart for animals."

"More like a soft spot in your head, but go on."

A big smile came to Roger's face. "Well anyway, me and the wife went to a party at a country club near the college I worked at. It was a swanky place. When we entered the event room, we saw a woman in a dress that covered little with a small dog in the very ample cleavage of her breasts which I suspected were artificial seeing as they were the size of Volkswagen Beetles. The dog was a Yorkie, but she could have fit a full grown

German shepherd between them. The dog was just as neurotic as any dog that size is. Really, I know for sure because I watched it closely till my wife made me stop."

"Roger, you're a dirty old man."

Roger smiled from ear to ear. "Nah, just a dog lover."

"Right," Bill said and stretched his answer out. "That's a funny story. Got a serious one now?"

"Yeah, I had a colonoscopy two years ago."

"Why? Roger, you're too young for those," Bill said.

"Colon cancer runs in the family. My father had it at a young age and had lots of problems. I got my checkup early just in case. It all went well, except they found a couple of polyps and removed them. They told me I needed to be aware of the problems and to get regular checkups which I do."

"What was it like?" Bill asked. "I mean, it's not exactly something us guys usually like to think about. You know, having something stuck up the old yang-yang."

"No, it's not," Roger said. "To say the least, I was nervous. On the day before my colonoscopy, I had to begin 'The Procedure.' No solid food, nothing but broth, and then that evening you take the Maximove. You get two batches of powder to mix in a liter bottle. When you drink it, it seems more like gallons. It took me an hour and it tasted and I think I'm being kind, like sheep spit and toilet bowl cleaner with a hint of lemon-lime. The instructions, which had to be written by a sicko comedian, said to expect a loose, watery bowel movement.

"That was the understatement of the year. I felt it coming and ran to the bathroom. I felt like the space shuttle trying to launch. I wished the toilet had a seat belt and a shoulder harness. I spent the next several hours confined to the bathroom. Everything in you goes, and when you think you're totally empty, you gotta drink another liter mixture, and then you travel into the future and crap out things you haven't even eaten yet.

"You try to get some sleep and hope it's all over. Often it's not. The next morning I went to the hospital. Nurse Ellen put an IV in my arm, and they started the happy juice. She told me some people mix whiskey or even vodka in their Maximove to help it go down. At first, I was mad I hadn't thought of that, but then I wondered if it was really a good idea. I can't imagine being blitzed when the Maximove kicked in like a dragster off the line. I could just see me staggering around trying to make it. Why, failure would have meant burning the whole bathroom, maybe the whole house."

"Please stop," Bill said. "My sides are splitting. I don't think I've ever laughed so hard."

"Well, it's a funny story, at least after it was all said and done. And it all came out well and ended well."

"Pun intended, Roger?"

"Pun intended and the doctor gave me a clean bill of health. He said to come in and just get regular checkups like we all should anyway. Come back sooner if I had any problems."

"That's funny. You made the best of a bad situation. A merry heart does a body good."

"Yeah Bill, I've heard that somewhere before. I was sure glad I had Kay, family, and her church friends for support during that difficult time. I really miss her and my kid. Since their deaths, it's been cave times."

"Cave times? You're gonna have to explain what you mean by that."

"Remember King David in the Bible?" Roger said.

"Yeah, took Israel to a world power long ago."

"It wasn't all roses in his life, Bill. He had 'cave times' as

Kay's pastor would have called it. David was down to nothing. He was alone in a cave lamenting. It's recorded in Psalms 13 and somewhere in one of the books of Samuel. No family, no mighty men followers, nothing, and King Saul's and his army are in hot pursuit wanting to kill him. It was the lowest point in David's life. I've felt like David since they died. The only time I've felt like my life had any purpose since then was when I worked on the Windover case, and I'm getting that feeling again now. Thank you for giving me a little reason to live."

Bill looked a little surprised. "You're welcome."

"I remember the sermon that day," Roger said. "I asked myself what would I do if I was in David's shoes or sandals, which would be more accurate. At that time, someone from the nursery came and got Kay. The baby was fussing up a storm, and mommy was needed. She left. I was all alone in a crowd. It frightened me, and I hoped it never happened."

Roger paused. "The pastor went on to tell about being on a flight that was in danger of crashing from severe turbulence. It went up and down like a roller coaster out of control. He hoped the pilot was a good one. He asked who the pilot of your life was. He said the Lord was like the hound of heaven pursuing us."

"Hope he was referring to a bloodhound, not a wolf type. One is so friendly; he'll lick you to death. One will eat you alive," Bill said.

"He mentioned a bloodhound. His words have rung in my ears at times over the years." The men said nothing for a few minutes. Roger broke the silence, "Think I'm ready for my nap now."

"Okay. One more thing while I'm thinking about it before you drift off," Bill said. "Will you report what you've found out for us? I'd like to try to stay out of interaction with Hernandez as much as possible. Seems my presence in the matters of this case is difficult and no point in making it more so. And I think she's been tracking down Missy's ex and trying to get an interview arranged with you."

"Good to hear she's thinking ahead," Roger said. "I like that.

"Now get your nap."

"Sure. I would if you'd shut up and please, no more stories. Not sure my ribs can take any more of your tales at this time."

"Ten-four, good buddy."

As Roger drove on down the interstate highway, Bill drifted off to sleep. Roger looked over at the sleeping man. *Sure hope what I find doesn't implicate him, but I've got to go where the facts lead. And he knows I will.* Roger sighed. There were times he didn't like police work.

# CHAPTER 13

Bill woke up and looked around? "Where are we?"

Roger said, "Well, Rip Van Winkle, we're almost to Florida. You slept a good two hours."

"Really? I didn't sleep very well last night. I need another pit stop. How about you?"

"Yeah, me too. I was thinking of stopping at the welcome station even if you hadn't woke up."

"Hey Roger, there's a Sonny's Barbeque restaurant at Exit 3. Stop there. My treat. You could use a break and it's getting close to lunch. We could beat the crowd."

"Now that's an offer I can't refuse, especially from an old skinflint like you."

"Roger, you cut me to the quick, but I forgive you just the same."

"Thanks, old buddy."

Bill grinned. "And I didn't kiss you last night if you're wondering. The only female that would kiss that face is your dog."

"Very funny, but I' let that crude comment slide seeing as how you're paying for my meal, ole buddy."

Ten minutes later, the men were sitting in a booth at the restaurant. As Bill was picking up the tab, he ordered for both of them, two rib platters with baked beans, French fries, toasted bread, and two beers which they were carded on to their amazement. The waitress told them everybody gets carded, Georgia law. She got the beers for them and left. More people were coming in. Several were men and women wearing law enforcement uniforms. After scanning the room carefully, they took a table in the far corner with their backs to the walls.

Bill said to Roger, "You can always tell who the cops are by their behavior even when they're not in uniform."

"So why ain't we sitting in the corner like them?"

"Nobody knows us here. Drink your beer I bought and enjoy."

"Thanks for the meal. Hope it doesn't come back to cost me too much in the future."

Bill grinned, "You never know. So tell me some things you've learned in your forensics/criminology/archaeology career that would add to my knowledge of the subjects and also you."

"Well Bill, I'm not really sure how much you know so pardon if I repeat something you already know."

"Okay, you're forgiven."

"You're in an awful forgiving mode today."

"And generous. You forgot generous."

"And generous." Roger stopped. "Will there be any more comments from the peanut gallery, or can I go on?"

"You better remember the peanut gallery is buying you lunch."

Roger grimaced. "Never mind. Now, where was I before I was so rudely interrupted? Oh yeah, my career. It started out with a call from the local police where I live up north. Someone at the college had suggested my name to them, and they gave me a call on a case they had. I helped where I could, and before long I was getting calls from every agency in the area. Several times I had to testify in court on criminal matters. I developed a good reputation for being thorough and honest. It was one of the things that helped me from getting steamrolled and rail-roaded by the administration at the college when they wanted me gone. Little did they expect me to fight back, but I knew how to hit them where it hurt. I got the word out what they were doing, and a lot of big contributions started to dry up, but that's another story."

"Yeah, a good reputation is worth its weight in gold."

"Very true, "Roger said. "It is. Whether it's a crime scene or an archaeological site, I try to 'read' it and 'listen' to it. I try to get a mental picture of what the whole would look like before looking at the pieces. You got to find and accurately record your findings whether it's bloodstains or a piece of ancient pottery. With criminology, there's more of a psychological angle trying to figure motive, behavior, and traits that will help in interpret-ing the evidence, although I like to imagine what the people in the ancient site were like also. I trust the old sites more. On a crime scene, you may have witnesses that are often less than reliable, and some of the physical evidence may be tainted or removed by the criminal. In either case, the main concern is to preserve the evidence and handle it properly."

"Now that's a nugget of truth. I can see why they kept coming back to you for help."

"Thanks, Bill. With crime, you always must assume that whoever was at the scene left something behind, or took some-thing away, or both. You work with what you have and look for the rest. Ever heard of Dr. Edmond Locard?"

"The name does sound familiar," Bill said. "I think he was mentioned in one of the criminology classes I took at the com-munity college. French guy if I remember right."

"He was. He said, 'Every contact leaves a trace.' In Lyons, France back in 1910, he started the world's first forensic laboratory. A man named Emile Gourbin was accused of strangling his mistress. He had an alibi, but Locard scraped beneath the man's fingernails and found skin flakes covered with face powder like the victim wore. Gourbin confessed to the crime. A more modern example would be right here in Florida. Ted Bundy was convicted of his last murder because of fibers transfer to his victim, some on her from his car and some on her clothes from him. Do you know if anything of this nature was looked at in this case?"

"I don't remember it being in the case summary," Bill replied. "Maybe the coroner would know or remember. I'll volunteer this – they checked my nails and found her skin cells, but I did check her neck for a pulse."

"The coroner keeps coming up. I need to see Will Corbett and see what he has," Roger said.

"You do."

Roger continued, "With evidence, you can draw conclusions and make connections. You have to keep the scene or site controlled. Access must be restricted to avoid contamination. Too many feet can destroy evidence on floors or the ground. Evidence can be found anywhere, door knobs, light switches, under furniture, and embedded in walls. Odors can give clues. Are the room's blinds drawn? Has the mail and newspaper been picked up? How fresh is the food in the refrigerator? Does it appear the scene has been cleaned up? Is there any unique evidence? Look for fingerprints or footprints and keep control of the evidence at all times."

"This case sure has had the ball dropped on the latter," Bill noted.

Roger said, "It has, and that's what's gonna make it so hard to prove, let alone get a conviction if we find the killer."

Bill nodded his head, but said nothing.

The waitress showed up with their meals in her hands.

"Sorry about that, fellows. The cook put your order behind the cops over there. They were in a hurry, and the cook owed them a favor, too."

Roger and Bill looked at the cops who looked back and nodded acknowledging the other men.

The waitress said, "And to make up for it, for you two and you two alone, it's an early happy hour. You get two for one beer. I'll be right back with them." She left and quickly returned with them. "Here you go."

"Thanks," Roger and Bill said in unison. She left, and they tore into the meal like hungry wolves. "This is really good, "Roger said. "Got any of these down our way, Bill?"

"Yup. You can trust me. I know where all the good eatin' places are. I don't do a whole lot of cooking, and when I do, it's usually opening a can and warming it."

"Why am I not surprised?"

Bill laughed, took a big swig of beer, and went back to devouring his meal. It didn't take them long to finish. The waitress brought the check, they left a nice tip, paid at the cash register, and were out the door. Standing by Bill's vehicle was the local police who they'd seen inside, and they were waiting. "This your vehicle?" the biggest one said.

"It's mine? Is there a problem?" Bill said.

"Your tag expired two months ago."

"No way," Bill said. "I always send a check in when the notice comes in the mail."

The biggest one said, "Well, you better look again. It's expired."

Bill looked, and sure enough, it was expired. "Well, I'll be. You're right."

"I need to see your driver's license and registration."

"Sure," Bill said and he got them along with his Chief of Police badge.

The big fellow looked at them. "So you guys are cops from Florida?"

"That's correct. We were up in South Carolina getting information on a cold case. We got hungry and stopped here. Thanks for letting me know about the tag. I'll get it taken care of immediately when I get back home. You gonna give me a ticket?"

The big guy said, "Nah, not for another man in blue. Mistakes happen. I'll let it go, but you do need to take care of it ASAP. What kind of case were you investigating?"

At that time, Roger spoke. "We were looking into a cold case. About five years ago, a young woman was brutally murdered at a diner in Titusville near the Space Center."

"Murder you say? We just had one here less than a week ago. We got a Jane Doe chillin' at the morgue. She was strangled and stabbed and the damnest thing was, the sicko who did this cut off one of her nipples."

"Interesting and sounds like the body was fresh," Roger said. "Sounds similar to our case. How about we exchange information and check back with each other? There could be a connection."

The big fellow said, "She was fresh. A kid stumbled on her. Like to scared him to death. Sure I'd like to keep in touch." He pulled a business card from his wallet and gave one to Roger and one to Bill. "This here's normally a quiet area. This is our first murder in about five years. We're not a big force, so we do it all."

They looked at the big man's card. "Sheriff Robert Twigg," Bill said.

"Yeah, that's me, and these people are all the officers in

blue for this county. It's big, and we're spread kinda thin."

Bill handed him his Canaveral Flats Chief of Police card. Roger said, "I'm new with the force and haven't had time to get cards. I'll write my name and number on the back of Bill's card," and he did.

The Sheriff said, "This sure was a surprise meeting you guys like this. I'll make sure we keep in touch. Like you said, the murders could be connected. And take care of that expired tag, y'all."

Bill said, "I will, and we'll be sure and keep in contact."

The Sheriff said, "Good. Now you guys have a nice day and drive safe. I've had to scrape too many people off the highway lately."

"We will," Roger said.

Roger and Bill got in their vehicle as the Sheriff and his crew drove off. Bill was driving, and he merged into light traffic on I 95 southbound.

Roger looked at Bill and said, "I have some questions for you, some serious and some not so serious. You game?"

"Sure. Begin."

"First off, where were you about a week ago?"

# CHAPTER 14

"Well, my first knowledge of this poor Jane Doe's demise was just a few minutes ago if you think I had anything to do with it. Secondly, about a week ago I was sick and took two days off from work. Guess I ate something that did not agree with me. I had diarrhea for the better part of those two days, and if you want proof, well, I flushed it away. I hope that's satisfactory for you, Roger."

"It will have to do for now, Bill. It just seemed suspicious and odd."

"Life can be like that. Aren't you the one who keeps telling me to keep an open mind and not get tunnel vision?"

"I am. Ockham's razor which we often use to solve problems tells us the simple solution is usually the right one," Roger said.

"Okay, gather all the facts and then come to a conclusion. Fair enough?"

"Fair enough."

The two men said nothing as the miles passed driving through the low country.

Roger yawned and said, "Bill?"

"What?"

"Do you understand women?"

Bill rolled his eyes. "No, I'm not even sure God understands them, and He made them."

"It used to be oh, so simple in the good old days before I met Kay."

"How so?"

"Take relationships," Roger said. "Before her, when I listen to a woman, I was trying to solve an important question. How was I going to get her to have sex with me? How was I going to get her naked?"

Bill nodded. "I can relate to that. Men see a problem and want to solve it."

"With her, it was different. She helped me see women as people, a different kind of people, but as real people, not just a set of breasts and the other goodies. The sex? With her, it wasn't just making love like all the others. It was love, real love, heart to heart love."

"Wish I could have met this wonderful woman."

"She changed me. She was fun to be around and complimented me. As I say, the lovemaking was great. Not only was the purpose pleasure, but you can make babies. She described it as an amazing gift from God. She said it united a husband and wife physically, spiritually, and emotionally. She was right. She asked me if I ever thought of the other women I'd been with. I told her, yes, but I tried not to. I remember her saying something about how you can't 'unglue' something. Soul ties she called it. I remember her saying God gave guidelines for sex and other things to protect us, not punish us. Sex has to be one of the best ideas God created for men and women to enjoy."

"No argument there and probably one of the most misused and abused," Bill said.

"True. Anything can be misused by someone with evil on their mind. This truck we're in doin' a great job by getting us from here to there, but it can also be used to mow people down."

"Yup, evil does things like that. It's why we need cops and

judges to be agents of justice."

"You know, Bill, even those I tried not to compare her to past lovers I struggled. Some of the memories are slow to fade and maybe even unforgettable."

A little grin came to Bill's face, but he said nothing. Seconds that seemed like hours passed before he spoke. "Wish I could have met her. From the way I can see she affected you, she must have been some woman."

"She was. There's a hole in my heart the size of Texas. How did I ever get here? This sure isn't the life I had dreamed of – not even close. Wish life had a reset button. Wish I had a magic wand and could somehow change things."

"Roger, I'm not much on God or religion or philosophy, but I know a few things. Want to hear some free advice for what it's worth?"

"Sure."

"Life is like a bicycle," Bill said.

"Life is like a bicycle?"

"Yup. Life is like a bicycle."

"That's it, Bill? Life's like a bicycle."

"Yup. You need to keep moving forward. If you don't, you fall over and crash. I know Kay and your son were an important part of your past, but it will drive you crazy thinking on what can't be undone. This life is full of disappointments. Things turn out vastly different than we could have ever imagined, and to be completely honest, not what we believe we deserve. My advice and I know it's easier said than done is to weep deeply over the life you hoped for. Mourn for your loss. I know it stings and absolutely hurts like hell. You have a choice. You can wallow in your problems, or make a deliberate decision to refocus and move forward. Embrace the life you have like a lost friend you've found again. Live for the now, not longing for the past you can't ever have again. Move forward out of the wasteland and count the blessings of today.

"Roger, we all know we're gonna die. Nobody gets out of this life alive. It's terminal. Live while you are alive. A lot of people think they have forever on this planet. Why not live like you died, had come back, and all this is extra?"

Roger rubbed his chin, "That sounds like something my wife would say to me."

"I'll say it again, wish I could have met her."

"I think you two would have hit it off just fine," Roger said.

Roger and Bill said nothing as mile after mile sped by. Bill looked at his watch. "You know, we just might miss the worst of Jacksonville rush hour traffic. Hope there's no accidents."

"Or road construction."

"Fat chance of the latter," Bill said. "They started rework on that road right after it was finished decades ago and will probably still be working on it the day the world ends."

"Government job."

"Yup. Government job," Bill said.

"Wonder what been going on while we were gone? Wonder if there's anything new on this case waiting for us when we get back?" Roger said.

"I have a feeling there is. I think we have enough pieces of this puzzle to get some idea of the overall picture."

"Let's put them together when we land and see what we got."

"That sounds like a doable plan," Bill said.

# CHAPTER 15

Roger looked off at a large field by the side of the road. "Isn't that cotton growing over there?"

Bill looked. "Yeah, I think it is. What of it?"

"Reminds me of my wife."

"You lost me on that, good buddy. You're gonna have to explain."

"The slaves used to pick cotton back in the bad old days."

"True," Bill said. "Don't want to return back to them either."

"My wife, Kay, used to call it America's 'peculiar institute.' She said it was a term slave owner's used to cover up the diabolical nature of slavery. You know I told you how we ended up getting married. Our unplanned pregnancy moved things along. It wasn't the ideal start, but I'm so glad we did it, and abortion wasn't an option for her. The college wanted groupthink, and when I really began to think, they couldn't have that. Teens aren't the only ones facing peer pressure to conform. With all the madness going on with the administration trying to get rid of me at the college, she and our young son were the one thing I could count on to bring me joy in those troubled times. I'm so glad we chose life. I'm so glad we didn't listen to some of the advice about 'choice' and 'women's health.' I'm so glad she believed our unborn child had a right to live."

"So Roger, how are slavery and abortion connected?"

"Several ways. Our government sanctioned both. Both dehumanized human life. Under slavery, blacks were seen as unhuman or lesser humans. You could ship them like cattle like Hitler did, deprive them of basic human rights, and treat them as objects of ownership. They were looked upon as an inferior life form. Politicians made bold assertions of the economic benefits of slavery.

"Today, the unborn child is referred to as a mass of cells, fetal tissue, and embryos rather than more humanizing alternatives. They talk about the rights of the mother and ignore the rights of the child, and both end up being harmed. The deaths of millions have been normalized by thinking of them as less than human. Some pundits even say abortion is merciful by preventing poor children from facing the grave struggles of life. Slave owners did the same when they pointed out the economic woes of freed blacks."

"That's some pretty heavy thought, Roger."

"I'll get off my soapbox in a minute, but I need to finish. Millions of unborn humans have been killed for the convenience of those already blessed with life. The great irony is too that this injustice of abortion affects the black community the worst. In some cities, more black children are aborted than born. There is no greater gift than life. We commit crimes slavers would have balked at, and the eugenicists like Margaret Sanger cheered, and they still do. She referred to blacks as 'weeds.' People like her believe we own life and can do with it as we want. Old Charley Darwin described the black man as less evolved and subhuman savages. Sound familiar?"

"It does," Bill said.

"I'm so glad we chose life. The time I spent with my son and wife were the happiest days of my life. It's what kept me sane when I was being railroaded at the college. I often think on what could have been, and I get depressed, and I drink too much."

"Roger, I don't know what I can do to help."

"Then just hear me out. I miss them so much. I would rather have died than them." He paused. "It makes me feel good that there are people alive today because of her. She volunteered at a crisis pregnancy center and was more than willing to share about her unplanned pregnancy. She was able to talk many young women into choosing life for their unborn child. She also counseled those that had abortions. She was so full of compassion, not the ire and judgment they expected. Every abortion has two victims. She was so understanding. Some young children living today are part of her legacy. Some women who were contemplating suicide are alive today because of her. God, how I miss her."

Bill looked at Roger with sympathy. "I don't know what to say."

"Then say nothing and just listen to the words falling out of my heart. I'm about done. William Wilberforce, an Englishman, worked to see that black people were seen as humans deserving rights like everyone else. He helped bring on a paradigm shift stemming from an understanding of life as it was intended to be. He was ridiculed as an extremist, an idealist not in touch with reality. He was told his defendants weren't worth it. Didn't he care about the well-being of those who benefited from slavery? What about them? In the end, this short little man broke the back of one of history's most evil practices. I'm so glad slavery is no more. My wife and son convinced me abortion is a poor choice. I'm just happy for the time I had them. My wife was a good Christian woman."

Bill said, "So I guess she talked to you a lot about God and all that religious stuff?"

"She did. She was never preachy, but always seemed to be teaching me stuff as you call it. You see, before she became a believer and even though she had been raised in the church, she determined to study the evidence and then using her reasoning powers and intellect, analyze it for herself and come to a conclusion. She was determined to find the truth. I think that's why she was so patient with me. She saw I needed to follow the same route in this journey."

"So where are you now, Roger?"

"I trying to be very open-minded to the facts and give the Bible a fair hearing. I listened to what the preacher had to say. I sometimes read it and still do. I'm interested in learning about it rather than pronouncing judgment from a position of abject ignorance like I've seen many so-called open-minded, educated people. I wanted my journey untainted by some in our culture. I've seen so much unwarranted disdain and disrespect. Often I've seen a conceited assumption from the elite who believe the beliefs are a product of blind faith, bereft of reason and thinking. I haven't found that to be the case. Though I may not have it all figured out and am still a sojourner, I'm inclined to believe my wife was right. In the meantime, I'm gonna continue studying and searching for an answer."

"I can see why you are so good at ferreting out an answer to a problem."

Roger said, "Yes, I've been told that is one of my strong points. I believe in high standards. I can't tell you how many times I've seen the results of biased, poor work. Researchers ignore conflicting data that doesn't go along with their assumptions. That gives junk science. Police investigations with predetermined outcomes produce wrongful convictions. Journalists who cherry-pick facts and distort images to support an agenda. Our media can become nothing more than a device for mass misinformation and manipulation usually using emotions. Factual errors, logical flaws, and significant omissions always produce bad results."

"Very true."

"Bill, do I ever miss her. When all that crap was going on

at the college, when all I heard was criticism and mocking, and it got me down, she was there. She was my cheerleader. She'd lift me up when I was discouraged. She kept telling me that some good would come from all this. It knocked the wind from my sails when she and my son died. I knew the desperation of a becalmed sailor in the middle of an endless ocean."

Bill hesitated. "Mind if I ask you a really hard question?"

"No, go ahead."

"Why haven't you blamed God for what's happened to you and turned your back on Him?"

A ponderous expression came to Roger's face. "That is a hard question Bill, but it deserves an answer. It would have been so easy to say how would a loving God do this to me? Why me?"

"And your answer is...?"

Roger said, "Life happens, to the just and unjust. This world has some great things and some horrible things. Seems like in everyone's lifetime, we all are the other guy who's had bad things happen from time to time. That's just the way it is. It rains on the good and the bad just the same. I have to admit sometimes I felt like Job's wife. You remember old Job and his wife in the Bible? She told him, 'Curse God Job and die.' His response in his misery said it all, 'Shall I accept good things from God, but not the bad also?' Job believed God was in this somehow even though he didn't understand. Just the same, he'd trust in his God. In time he'd understand." Roger paused. "There have been days I've felt like ending it all, but somehow, I feel and know sometime I'll understand. In the meantime, I drink to ease the pain."

Bill glanced at Roger. "You look like a burden just rolled off your back."

"Yeah, it's hard to talk about, and when I do, it wears me out. You good with driving some more? I think a nap would refresh me at this time."

"Go ahead. I'm good. Catch some shut eye. And glad I asked for the abridged version."

Roger laughed. "Be glad I'm sleepy. Don't tempt me to get on my soapbox."

Bill rolled his eyes. "You, on a soapbox? No way. I can't image that."

They both laughed.

Bill said, "Oh, while I'm thinking about it, there's a retired fellow in Canaveral Flats, I believe you'd like to talk to sometime. His name's Dr. Jones. He was a missionary in some country where there was a lot of persecution. I remember him saying, 'Whatever happens, just or unjust, pain or pleasure, compliment or criticism, you take it into the purpose of your life and make something out of it. It becomes part of your story, your testimony.'"

"He sounds like an interesting character. Thanks," Roger said.

"Our little town's filled with interesting characters. I can assure you of that." Bill laughed at his own joke. "One last question, in a nutshell, tell me your philosophy of life as you see it now."

"Bill, I'm glad you want the nutshell version. My eyes are getting droopy. Well, let's see. Family is important. Work hard. Have honor. I believe in law and order. I can't see how this world was created by nothing. Something had to do it. All life is important. Don't take it for granted and don't destroy innocent life. Truths exist as sure as the sun rises in the east. It doesn't change with the whims of society. Some of the biggest fools I have ever met were on college campuses. Facts are facts and to some who say they are most tolerant and accepting; they're blind to the fact they're not, and they will try to shut you up when you point their folly out. But I have a big streak of stubborn and will continue doing what's necessary to find the whole truth, no matter how unpopular some of my findings might be with some people. I'm a truth seeker, and the truth can be hard and uncomfortable. Often it's like an alarm bell goes off in my head when things get too comfortable and I wonder why. That good enough?"

"Yeah, that's a lot of cud to chew on. Should keep me awake while you catch some shut-eye."

Roger curled up in the seat best he could and soon was fast asleep and snoring softly.

Bill looked at his sleeping companion and smiled. Yes, he had chosen wisely. Roger was the right man for what he wanted.

# CHAPTER 16

Five years ago at the Canaveral Diner

"You? How'd you get in here? I told you I never wanted to see you again, Love," she snarled and emphasized the last word. "Get out. Get out now!"

Those were the last words she ever spoke. She heard a clicking sound and fell to the ground. She moaned as pain rocked her body. Helpless, she watched as the man pulled a bottle from his jacket and poured some of its contents on a rag which he then held covering her nose and mouth. He watched as her eyes closed and her breathing became slower. She stirred, and he put more liquid on the rag which he returned to her face. Each time he did this; her breathing slowed and finally came to a stop. He smiled, but she'd died too soon before the real fun had begun. No matter.

Carefully, he removed her clothing one piece at a time and placed them neatly in a pile nearby. He sneered as he mounted her dead body. The words, "Oh, this is so good," slipped from his lips as he climaxed.

He pulled his pants back up and tightened his belt. A look around the kitchen area told him where the knives would be. A particularly wicked looking one called him. *Use me.* He picked it up in his gloved hand. The first thrust into her heart yielded little blood. *Yes, she was dead.*

He smiled cruelly as rage filled him. Twenty-three times

he stabbed her. He counted every one. His anger was spent after the first eighteen strokes, that and the fact the tip of the knife had broken off. No matter. The last five were just because he could and wanted to. He had his reason. He laid the bloody knife on the counter where it could be found.

Her blood trickled across the tile floor along the crack and ran into the floor drain. *Pity, it had to end like this.* He felt a twinge of sorrow as he looked at her naked body with her legs spread wide. He'd leave her like this. He wanted to remember her this way. It seemed only a fitting end. Oh, and he needed something to remember her by.

Satisfied, he tiptoed around the corpse and the blood trail coming from it. He looked out the peephole of the service door and saw the coast was clear. He quickly exited and locked the door behind him. A devious thought came to him. Should he leave the key in the double cylinder deadbolt door lock? Why not? It would give the police something to think about. Was it important or a red herring? Yes, he would leave the key and see how it worked out.

The distant street light barely illuminated the back parking area. Quietly, he slipped across the lot and followed the path through the tangle of Brazilian Pepper trees to the Florida East Coast Railroad tracks. Anyone seeing him at this hour might write him off as a hobo or homeless man continuing his wandering to nowhere. A street crossed the tracks, and he took a left there and walked deliberately to his car in the Scotty's Lumber Yard parking lot.

The door creaked as he opened it and got in. He smiled as he thought of his deed tonight. He was satisfied he would not be found out. Only he would know what happened and why. How much would *Florida Today* have to say about his activities? How accurate would it be? What would they miss or leave out? No matter.

He heard the sound of an approaching train. Its bright

light hit the windshield as it rounded a slight curve and temporarily blinded him. As his eyes adjusted back to the darkness, he saw the last half of the long train pass with its cars full of heavy limerock.

He started the car, and its lights penetrated the night. He yawned and realized how tired he was. His first killing had left him pleased but exhausted. He'd sleep like the dead. A triumphant laugh escaped his mouth. Someone else was sleeping like the dead.

It has been so easy. Was it always this easy if you planned it right? He wondered and smiled.

Yes, he was tired. Maybe he'd skip work today. The world could get along without him for a day. It would get along without her. Taking a life had exhausted him, and he'd need time to recharge. No matter. She was dead, and he was free. That's what really mattered.

# CHAPTER 17

"Who's there?" the gravelly voice asked.

"Will Corbett, it's Roger Pyles of the Canaveral Flats Police Department wanting in. I need to talk to you."

"Oh, Roger. I'll buzz you in. Just a second."

Roger heard a clicking sound as the door unlocked. He walked in, went through a second door, and found himself in an office room. Will Corbett was sitting at a desk and working on some paperwork. He looked up and said, "Let me finish this report, and I'll be right with you. It won't take but a moment. Help yourself to some coffee and please put a lid on the Styrofoam cup. Can't tell you how much paperwork's been ruined by spilled coffee, including my own. I won't be long."

"Okay." Roger found the coffee on a small table near the wall. It was black as used motor oil like he liked it. He poured a cup, put a lid on it, took a sip, and sat down in a metal chair in front of the coroner's desk. "Good coffee, just like I like it, hot and black." He laughed at his own little inside joke, but Will paid him no mind. He was focused on the report.

Roger watched as Will worked his way down the page and signed his name at the bottom. "There," Will said. "Another mindless paperwork report sent from some anonymous bureaucrat who probably won't read it, and if he or she does, most likely won't understand it anyway. Just has to be done to satisfy some government requirement in a law written by pompous fools with no understanding of what people in my position do daily, but what else is new?"

Roger laughed. "So tell me how you really feel."

"You don't want to know. It's been one of those days. Seems like I've been filling out government forms all day just because I have to. I wish the idiots who implemented this would have to be held responsible for all the money they waste, money we could use to bring this place up to date. There're some advantages to working with the dead. They don't complain, don't give back talk, and don't demand you fill out foolish forms."

Roger let the rant pass. "You moved. Wish I'd called before I drove to Melbourne. I wanted to talk to you face to face and with no one possibly listening in."

"Yeah, we'd been in transition for some time. Only been totally moved in here for just a few days. The county finally agreed with me that I needed more modern facilities. This place has electrical backups and better security. The attempted break-in recently at the old facility was a small disaster. It sure messed with the bodies in the cooler. The perps got part way in, but not all the way. I got a good blood sample from the broken window, but so far, we haven't figured out who done it."

"Any idea what they were looking for?"

"Well, my guess would be it was either kids thinking a morgue would be fun, some ghoulish people with evil on their minds, some sick puppies, someone wanting to destroy evidence involving a body I had there, or maybe trying to get to some old files I keep locked up securely."

"No suspects?" Roger said.

"None. One advantage to this new place is it has video surveillance."

"That stuff's becoming more common."

"It is, but there's not too much of it around here yet. Still pretty expensive."

Roger said, "I got a question for you. Why'd they put this place in such an out of the way location in Rockledge? The road I took to get here, Murrell Road, has four lanes but no traffic. I could have lain down and taken a nap and not gotten run over."

"It's called planning. Some people want this area to look like South Florida, sprawl everywhere. They think that some-day soon this road will connect with several others and be full of traffic. Can't say I'm looking forward to that day, but I fear it's not far in the future."

"I hope you're wrong. I like it the way it's now."

"I do too. Maybe when it happens, I'll have enough years in to retire and move on to someplace less congested. What did you come here for today? Certainly not to hear about my com-plaints about idiots making work for others to justify their jobs and not to talk about traffic. What's on your mind, Roger?"

"I'm here about a cold case."

"Which one? We've got a goodly number to pick from."

"The murder of Missy McCoy."

"Doesn't ring a bell. Help me out."

"It was at the Canaveral Diner in Titusville about five years ago. Multiple stab wounds."

Will thought for a moment. "Oh yeah. Now I remember. There were some strange things about that case."

"How so?"

Will said, "Let me get the file and show you."

"You have a file on this? What I've got so far was very sketchy and incomplete. Seems a lot of the evidence at the Sher-iff's Department has gone missing."

"I'm not surprised. The security on that room was little to none existent. This county is growing so fast, the old ways that used to work, no longer are working or working poorly. The county and everything else in it is in catch up mode. Just last week, I heard of a church that discovered a long-term theft. Seems one of the members had found a way to skim from the offerings over more than a decade. Enough little anomalies hit the radar screen for them to hire a forensic accountant. He found the problem. The church's bookkeeping system was set up when the church was small. It worked then. The church now has over 1500 members and the old system was still in place and had a few loose ends the thief had found and had taken advantage of. The accountant quit counting when he found over one million dollars missing."

"That's an incredible story," Roger said.

"It is, and the Sheriff's Department is just as vulnerable along with lots of other private and public entities. I've seen some things here I'd rather not talk about, and I know it happens everywhere. Let me quit jawing and get the file."

"Okay."

Will left the room. Roger could hear what sounded like a heavy metal door open. He took a sip of coffee. About a minute later, he heard the door shut and also the sound of a heavy lock locking. Will appeared with a file in his hand. "Here we go. Everything I have on the Missy McCoy case."

The two men took a quick look at the contents of the file. Roger asked, "How is it you have this? The evidence department had next to nothing."

"I'm not surprised at all. Like I said, things around here haven't kept up with the times and need to change. I keep a duplicate file of everything I have and everything I can get from the investigations by the Sheriff's Department. I'm not sure they knew I have this backdoor access, but I do. The system works both ways. There are times the county forgets to tell me things on a timely basis and other times they forget they send me things that maybe they shouldn't."

"Will, you do know about Agent Gloria Hernandez?"

"Can't say the name is familiar. She a cold case murder victim too?"

"No," Roger said. "She's the new person who's responsible for looking into cold cases and forensics at the Sheriff's Department. Just came up here from Miami PD. She's the one who gave me the little she had on the case I was asked to look into. What you have here is a gold mine. Do you have this on each case you handle?"

"There are a few records that the Brevard County Sheriff's Department didn't send over, but yeah, I've got a substantial file on nearly all of them. Are you thinking what I'm thinking?"

"Yes, I am. Someone found out about this file or another like it you have and doesn't want the evidence to see the light of day. Will, I think you need to add even more security to your new facility here in Rockledge. If word gets out that you have this much evidence in one spot, you're going to be a target for a lot of low-life criminals who'd let little or nothing stop them from destroying this evidence that could tie them to the crimes they, so far, have gotten away with."

"Tell you what Roger; I can make photocopies of this file for you. I'm not breaking any rules because you as a cop and an investigator of this crime have the authority to have them and need them to do your job."

"You do that, please. I'll wait. I can go over them slowly and thoroughly and see what I can find. You never know what will happen when you start turning over rocks."

"True," Roger replied. "And be careful. A lot of the creatures under rocks don't like the exposure and will strike out at you."

"Very true. I'll remember that. Some people think of

Florida as a tropical paradise, but from what I read of Eden, even that original paradise had an evil snake."

"Let me get those copies for you." Will went to the photocopier. Roger watched as Will moved the setting to fine quality. One by one, the machine ran the pages through it. It clicked and buzzed as it performed the task it was made to do. Several minutes passed as it worked. The task completed, Will got a manila envelope and placed the pages in it. He handed it to Roger. "Here you go. Hot off the presses."

Roger took the file. "You weren't kidding. These are hot."

"Yeah, it's an older machine I got from County Surplus. They were going to sell it, but I got it. It's slow, noisy, and produces a lot of heat as it works, but this old model produces a quality copy better than any the county buys now. I was lucky to find it. I could use the money allotted to this department for something else I need or needed more."

"Like more security?" Roger said.

"Yup, like more security and maybe less unnecessary paperwork. I'll look into more security today. Any suggestions?"

Roger thought and smiled. "Maybe a junkyard dog?"

"Not a bad idea, but I may have to clean up dog messes every day. And a bored dog can create a lot of problems. Let me think about it."

"Where I was a professor," Roger said," the school's greenhouse had a mouse problem, and no amount of spray or poison could get rid of the mice. A stray cat showed up, and the mouse problem got smaller and smaller. An employee got the smart idea of listing the cat as 'biological pest control' in their expenses, and that was good enough for the bean counters, and the cat food was now paid for, and it was cheaper and better than the exterminator service they had been paying for." And they named the cat after the college president, Harlow.

"That's a funny story," Will replied. A thoughtful look crossed his face. "Junkyard dog? I'll think on it. I do believe I'm going to need something more than I have now."

"I think you're right. I'll look at this report and get back with you if I need anything more," Roger said.

'Please do. Details of the case are coming back to me. It would make my day if I could help you find the SOB that committed this crime."

"Thanks. I'll do that." Roger turned and went out the first glass door. The outside door was locked. Roger turned to Will who got the hint. The door buzzed and Roger let himself out. As he walked to his vehicle, he pondered. Somewhere in the file he held could very well be the clue that solved this case. Somewhere, if only he could find it. Justice for a young woman depended on it.

# CHAPTER 18

Roger reclined in his new La-Z-Boy chair. He sipped at a beer as he examined the cold case papers the coroner had provided him with. He hoped there was something that would jump out at him, something so obvious it had been missed all this time, but he could find nothing hiding in plain sight. The only thing that had jumped around today had been the stray cat that had found her way in the doggy door and been eating the dog's food. The call of nature had beckoned him, and when he returned, there was the cat. She was running and jumping all over the porch as she tried to find her way out. It was cats gone wild. K9 eyes curiously followed the panicked cat as she frantically sought to escape. The cat rushed out the screen door like she was rocket propelled when Roger had opened it. She made her escape, and she bolted into some nearby vegetation.

He looked up from his task as an old pickup came down the lane to his old trailer. He recognized the vehicle. It belonged to Bill Kenney. Roger wondered what he wanted and wasn't sure he wanted to know, but was certain he was about to find out. Hook or crook was sly ole Bill's modus operandi. He usually got what he wanted even from the unsuspecting.

Bill got out of his truck and headed to the screened in trailer porch. He carried something in his left hand. "Hello, Roger. About time you got up. It's about the crack of noon."

Roger growled, "I've been up for hours looking at these papers. Haven't you got anything better to do, flatfoot, than bother an honest law abiding citizen?"

"Remember, it was me who pulled those strings and got you and Tom out of those numerous possible charges not too long ago. Remember?"

"How could I forget? You won't let me. I'm beginning to wonder if it wouldn't have been better to go to jail than have to listen to you as you hold it over my head." He stopped. "What do you want anyway?"

"Have anyone told you that you look and sound like Sam Elliott after an all-night bender?"

Roger rolled his eyes. "State your business before I call the cops."

"I am the cops."

"I am too, and you won't let me forget it. As I said, what do you want? I'm starting to get irritated."

Bill said with great sarcasm, "I hadn't noticed."

If Roger could have chewed nails, he'd have spit them as bullets at Bill.

"Had lunch yet?"

"No."

"Hungry?"

"Yes."

"I got you a Happy Meal. Thought you could use it."

Roger frowned. "The McDonald's bag kinda gave it away. Free food is free food even if it comes from you. I know there's a catch. What do you want?"

"Just to do a wellness check and see how the case was going."

Roger muttered something unpleasant under his breath and said, "I'm fine. Give me the food."

"I brought some for your dog too. Kind of payback for what she did in my truck."

"Oh no, you don't. I don't need that kind of a mess here."

Bill smiled, "Okay, I'll eat the meal."

Roger munched down on a French fry. "You had that planned out all along. You weren't gonna feed her. That was your lunch. You had no intention of feeding K9."

By now, Bill was grinning. "Why Roger, you cut me to the quick. To think I was capable of doing something like that." He sat on a chair next to Roger. "Did you get a cat?"

"No."

"Saw one when I came in."

"Yeah, there's been a stray hanging around. Been eating the dog's food."

"Doesn't that bother K9?"

"Don't seem to. Maybe she feels sorry for another lost creature. She was one too when I found her at the pound."

"Could be."

"What did the cat look like?" Roger said.

"Well, the streak that I saw looked like a mottled, black and gold tortoiseshell," Bill said.

"Yup, that's the one. I saw her hanging around. Actually, I heard her before I saw her. She was crying something fierce. Sounded lost and afraid. I talked to her, and she would cry back in a pitiful cry. I put a little food out in a bowl in the yard, and it's been disappearing. I forgot to tell Lester to put some out there too. He'd been feeding the dog when we were away, but you knew that."

"Old Lester, very dependable. When he says he'll do it, you won't have to worry about it getting done."

"Lester seems like a good guy."

"He is. So, you're feeding a cat? Sounds to me like you have a cat now. Once they find out you'll feed them, they make themselves at home. You've been warned."

"Bill, she's awful flighty and runs from me."

"Roger, trust me on this. Before long, she'll be running around like she owns the place and you too, especially a tortie. Once a cat like that claims you, it's all over. You're theirs. You'll soon learn about tortitudes."

"You mean like catitudes?"

"Yup, but ratcheted up about ten times. Torties are unique among cats."

"You make it sound bad, Bill."

"Not really. You won't find a more loving cat able to keep you entertained for hours. Think Tigger from the Pooh stories, a kitten, and a puppy all rolled into one, and that comes close to a tortoiseshell cat. Innocent and curious. A little flighty too."

"Interesting."

Bill said, "You need to set a trap."

Roger's eyes widened. "I couldn't do that. She's already scared enough."

"Not that kind of a trap. You said she already knows how to get in and at the food on the porch. Dog don't bother her. What you need to do is find a kitty size cardboard box and set it out. Works every time. And humane too."

Roger said, "You know you may have something there. That could work. A cat would be kinda nice to have around."

"Keep the vermin down."

"Vermin like you?" Roger said.

"Doubt it. Didn't work with K9."

"True. Wonder if she would sleep on my face."

"What?" Bill said. "That's crazy. Whoever heard of something like that?"

"Ever heard of the Furry Freak Brothers?"

"Can't say I have."

Roger said. "Guess you wouldn't. They were a series of underground comics that were popular on college campuses. Three hippies were living together and doing all kinds of wild and crazy things."

"Guess I missed them."

"One ole hippie, Fat Freddy, had a big yellow tiger cat with a real attitude that used to sleep on his face when he was asleep. It was one of the running jokes in the Freak Brothers comic books."

"Roger, I think you're safe from that happening. Let's eat our Happy Meals before they get cold. What are all these papers?"

"I got a copy of the whole report on Missy's death from the coroner."

"Really? The Coroner keeps copies? Care to tell me what you've found?"

"Okay, but doggone it. Let's eat first."

"Agreed."

The two men chowed down on the Happy Meal, a burger, fries, and a soft drink. Bill said, "Hope you like Coke,"

Roger growled in a low grating voice, "Shut up and eat."

Bill nodded, and the two ate away at the Happy Meals without further comment. When they were done, they put all the food containers in one bag and placed it in the trash. Bill said, "I'm pleasantly surprised you located a copy of the report.

Find anything helpful?"

"Yes, I'm working out a timeline for the events. I'm gonna figure out how everyone fits into this tale including you. Still no alibi and why not?"

"I have my reasons. You'll understand in the end."

"That's part of my plan. I'll follow up on the last week/day/hours of the victim, who she interacted with, possible suspects, etcetera. Somewhere in there is my answer."

Bill said, "That's usually the way it works."

"I'll look for gaps, inconsistencies, places where info is missing or seems out of place or places where something is squirrelly. You know, a detail that just doesn't pass the smell test."

"Like my lack of an alibi?"

"That's one, Sherlock. That's a big one."

"Care to share anything more, Roger? You know, I'd make a good sounding board."

"Not at this moment. I'm developing ideas right now, and it would be best if you stayed out of it for the meanwhile. I've still got a lot to do. The answer's in this report. All I have to do is what I just told you, and all will be cleared up."

"Just like in an Agatha Christie mystery?" Bill said.

"Somethin' like that. If I want or need your help, I'll get in touch. Anything else you want to tell me?"

"Got the house cleaned."

"Good. It looked like a pigsty when we got back from South Carolina," Roger said.

"Yeah, I ain't much of a housekeeper. Lester's sister was there all morning cleaning up. I can make a mess incredibly fast."

"It's a wonder she didn't refuse to do it or declared the place a public health hazard and have it burned to the ground."

"Now that ain't fair. I may not be a neatness nut, but I'm not Mr. Piggy either."

Roger said, "Just glad to hear it's now clean and you're not living like a filthy hermit."

"Thanks, ole buddy. You're a good one to talk. Hey, gotta go. Gotta keep Canaveral Flats safe from the forces of evil."

"You do that, and I'll let you know if I have questions. I probably will."

"Okay, and good luck with your cat," Bill said.

"I don't have a cat."

"Ah yes, you do. I can see it. Even Ray Charles could see that. Got to go. See ya."

Roger waved goodbye as Bill departed. He hopped in the truck and was soon out of sight.

Bill was correct. Somewhere in this report was the answer or a clue that would lead to the solution. All he had to do was see it. Right now, he was having a hard time reading the tea leaves. It was there, he was sure. Perhaps if he just did a little stirring of the pot, something would come into view, or it would get someone's attention. Sending a dog out in the field could flush a hunter's prey, and maybe his investigation would make someone nervous. Some scenarios were forming in his mind. It troubled him that Bill wouldn't provide an alibi and he seemed to have one, but it could be just a ruse. The report provided by the coroner was a Godsend. Nothing succeeds like persistence and a plan, and a picture continued to develop in Roger's mind.

He wondered about the cat. Would it play a part in this story? His dog, K9, had kept him from getting killed in the Windover investigation just like the Shaman had said. What was that strange fellow up to? Still out in the St. John River marsh living off the land? Still with his sidekick, Del? Still scaring the hell out of criminals and troublemakers out there? Still rescuing people in distress?

There were so many unanswered questions. What would life have been like if his wife and son hadn't died? What was he doing now? What was he here for? Why? Roger sighed as he thought. One thing he was sure of-he needed a reason to get up every morning and some daily routine. This investigation provided both. He could thank Bill for that. Old Bill, how did he fit? Were his motives as open as he'd like you to think, or was there more to it, or maybe even a little of both? Anyone, even he, in a moment of anger could snap and do something unimaginable. He'd seen it happen again and again. Roger knew this much for sure. He would follow this trail wherever it took him, and let the chips fall where they may. And that was elementary, my dear Watson. The game was afoot. Henry IV and Shakespeare would understand.

# CHAPTER 19

Roger laid stretched out in his La-Z-Boy. Its padding was already conforming to his lanky body. He read the files he'd acquired from the coroner on the Missy McCoy case again. He was getting a good grasp on what had happened and how the case had been handled, poorly, and he had some ideas on what his next steps would be. K9 slept peacefully nearby. She'd been up earlier needing attention, and Roger was more than happy to give it to her. He'd found an old stuffed Teddy Bear at Catholic Thrift Store nearby, bought it, and presented it to K9 for a play toy. She'd taken to it immediately and often carried around in her mouth. She was sleeping next to it now.

He watched as the tortoise-shell cat cautiously crept across in the less-than-manicured yard. Maybe he'd have Lester cut it and work on the fence. Good fences make good neighbors. They said, "Keep Out. Invited Guests Only." A good fence would also protect what he cared for.

The cat was looking better than she had when he first saw her some time ago. K9's food was putting some meat on her bones. She'd already been bringing him presents. Yesterday, he'd found a dead male mole in his yard. He knew it was a male because the corpse had an erection. What a way to die. The day before, he had found a young dying possum. It took two deep breaths and then was no more. She seemed to be quite a hunter. He guessed she had been living on her own for some time.

She looked around as she pussyfooted her way toward the screen door with the doggie door at the bottom in Roger's screened porch. Roger followed her movement with his eyes and barely breathed. She stopped at the little door, looked around carefully, and then nosed her way in, and headed for the waiting food. The cat eyed K9 and tiptoed to the food. She looked around one more time and then began to eat hungrily.

Roger watched as she rapidly ate. She raised her head and looked around. Her eyes froze on Roger's eyes, and they widened. Her body tensed and she began to back to the door. Her hindquarters touched it, and she deliberately slunk out the little door. She never took her eyes off Roger. The small door closed without a sound, and she turned to the woods. After walking about 20 feet, she halted, sat down, licked her fur, and returned her gaze to Roger. "Good kitty," he whispered. "Good kitty."

She seemed pleased with herself. Her head jerked around at a distant clamor that was growing louder. Dogs were barking and howling, and her ears were fixed on the approaching sound. She looked back at Roger who was now standing, but quickly returned her attention to the coming tumult. K9 remained sleeping.

From behind some brush growing in the ditch in the next lot, Roger saw a sight that made his jaw drop. A small wagon pulled by 6 goats headed down potholed Canaveral Flats Boulevard. The wagon looked like something Gypsies had discarded. It had pots and pans hanging from the sides clanking as the solid metal wheels hit the ruts, holes, and washboard sand. On top were a washtub, a wooden box, a large wicker basket, and a homemade sign that said, "PREPARE TO MEET THY GOD." Worn looking bungee straps held all tightly on the roof. Clothing, plastic jugs containing water, and other curiosities hung from the sides.

The goats baaed and bleated loudly as they passed. They were either white or black, but some were a mixture of both. Some had long horns, some short, and one had none. Over the noise, Roger heard a throaty, gravelly voice shout, "Onward Peter and Paul. Stay the course, James and John. Steady as she goes Thomas and Thaddeus. We're glory bound. Almost home."

A bald leathery man with a beard that Santa Claus would envy wore bib overalls that looked like they had been obtained from the dumpster behind a thrift shop. He looked at gawking Roger, smiled, and raised his hand to wave. He was missing several teeth. Almost without thinking, Roger raised his hand. He watched as the aberration continued on down the street. The clanging and bleating slowly receded as it passed from view. The cat who'd been watching the sight turned quickly back to Roger. He could tell she had been distracted and forgotten about him. "Good kitty," he said. "Good kitty." She thoughtfully looked at him for a few more seconds, licked her right front leg, and then walked into some nearby weeds and brush and disappeared.

Roger turned his attention to K9. "Some watchdog you are. You could sleep through a hurricane, maybe even the end of the world." She paid him no mind and continued sleeping. Roger sat back down and read some more in the cold case file. He pondered several things in his mind, one which made the acid level in his stomach rise.

A truck skidded to a halt on the unpaved road in front of his old trailer. K9 growled, but didn't open her eyes. "That's right, girl. It's your favorite cop again, the famous Canaveral Flats Chief of Police, Bill Kenney, and it looks like he's coming this way. I think the acid level in my stomach is gonna get some more sour if that's possible."

She growled again, a little louder this time. "Yeah," Roger said. "You took the words right out of my mouth."

Bill opened the dummy locked gate and rapidly headed toward the trailer. "Hey, Roger," he said as he barged past the man and dog and went into the trailer.

Roger grunted, "Why don't you make yourself at home?"

Some minutes later Bill returned with a cold beer in his hand. "Whoo-ee, did I have to go. Being a cop, sometimes you're too busy to go or in the wrong place and can't, and when you do, it's Katie bar the door."

"Bill, I hope you turned on the exhaust fan after you were done."

"I did, but it wasn't working. I was afraid to light a match as it could have blown us both to kingdom come."

"Thanks for that, old buddy. It wasn't on my schedule to die today especially from a friendly fire gas explosion." He stopped. "Know anyone who can fix a dead fan?" Roger asked.

"Check with Lester. Probably something simple and he's a good handyman jack of all trades kinda guy. Probably a loose wire, short somewhere, bad fuse, or maybe the fan has died. I'm sure he can figure it out and be really reasonable about the price too. Thanks for the beer."

"Yeah, why don't you help yourself?" Roger said. "Barge rights in here, stink up the place and help yourself to my beer. Aren't you on duty, Bill?"

"You know the drill. I check myself off the clock one microsecond before the can hits my lips and back in when the last drop slides down my gizzard."

"Thought that was the case for you, Bill. What do you want? Why don't you make yourself at home? Take a load off your mind and have a seat on my porch. You already sat on the throne."

"Roger, you should know by now if I enter your trailer, it'll be to get beer or use the bathroom 99% of the time?"

"And the other 1%?"

"Why that's when I put on my super suit and save Canaveral Flats and the world from all kinds of doers of evil."

"Should have known I'd get an answer like that," Roger said. "What's on your mind aside from my beer and bathroom, Mr. Superhero?"

Bill ignored the cut. "I haven't talked to you in a few days. We need to get each other up to speed on what's been going on. You know, compare notes and the like. What's up with you here?"

"Well, I think I may be losing my mind."

"Small loss if you want my opinion."

Roger gave Bill a nasty look. "No, I don't want your opinion, ole buddy. Don't give me that. You must have seen it too."

"Seen what?"

"The aberration. It just went down the road. You had to have seen it?"

"Okay, Roger. What did it look like?"

"A tumble down wagon pulled by six goats with an old man at the wheel. He'd made the Beverly Hillbillies look like bluebloods."

"Any other witnesses?"

"Just the stray cat."

"Not even K9?" Bill asked.

"No, K9 slept through the whole thing."

"How much have you been drinking, Roger?"

"Less than usual. Look, if you think it's the DTs, it ain't that. I know what I saw."

Bill smiled. "Yeah, I know what's going on."

"Well? Am I going crazy or not?"

"That's a question for a professional."

"Very funny, old friend."

Bill took a sip on his beer, swallowed, and said, "That was no aberration. That was Goatman."

"Goatman?"

"Yeah, Goatman. His real name is Charley Smith. He's some of that local color I was telling you about living in Canaveral Flats."

"Like you?"

"And you."

"I guess so." Roger sighed, "That's good to know. At least I'm not going crazy. You didn't have to lead me on like that, ole buddy."

"Just checking on your well-being like a good cop and friend, ole bud."

"Very funny. Ha ha."

"And I saw the cat too. They're both real. You feeding her?"

"Yeah," Roger said.

"Then you got a cat now."

"Just what I need, a cat."

"Yup. She'll make herself at home and won't leave no matter what. My theory is dogs had to be domesticated by ancient man, but cats just showed up and wouldn't leave. You got a cat."

"I think so, too."

"Besides," Bill said, "you're a homeowner. Look at the word homeowner. It's got the word meow in it. You got a cat."

"I believe you're right. Now tell me about this Goatman

fellow," Roger said.

"He got shot up in World War II. Army put him on full disability, so he gets a check each month. Got a cash settlement in the beginning for his service and used it to buy one of the first lots sold in Canaveral Flats. Fact is he's got two lots of about 3 acres each side by side in the back of Canaveral Flats. You think its primitive here in this section, you ain't seen nothing till you get out there. Think jungle."

"Lions and tigers and bears?" Roger asked.

"More like bobcats, Florida panthers, wild pigs, snakes, and gators. Don't think we have any bears, but there are a lot north of Orlando in the woods. As the city grows, human and bear contact is becoming more frequent, and it's usually not good for the bears."

"Oh my."

"Oh my is right," Bill said."Goatman had a woman people say was his wife. That was before my time when I came here. The story goes she got tired of him and his ways and left. I don't know what became of her. Like I said, before my time. Anyway, they had a son. He used to go with his dad on his travels in the goat wagon. That wanderlust urge would just hit him, and he'd take off for parts unknown and return when he got tired of traveling."

"Yeah, no place like home."

"The kid grew up, got tired of the primitive living, and joined the Army to escape. Last I hear, he was with some Special Forces group doing black ops type of work. Hush-hush stuff, you know."

"Okay, now I know about Goatman, and I'm not going crazy. What did you come here for besides the beer and bathroom?"

Bill took a sip on the beer. "By the way, thanks for the

beer."

"You're welcome," Roger growled. "Now, what did you really come here for?"

Bill said, "Funny you should ask. It's been an interesting few days. I wasn't feeling well and went to the doc. She looked at me, ran some tests, and said it was a cold, so you know, take Tylenol, get plenty of sleep, and if it didn't go away soon, come back for a dose of penicillin."

"With all your catting around, penicillin would be a good catchall."

Bill ignored Roger's remark. "She told me something in confidence that she would have to deny if it ever came up, but the local pastor at the Riverside Baptist Church may have some information that could help you in the investigation."

"Interesting."

"Go talk to him. He's a good guy. Used to be a Brevard County Deputy before the Lord got a hold on him. Also, I talked to Hernandez, got her up to speed on our trip. She said she wanted to talk to you."

"That's not a surprise," Roger said. "I've been wondering how long a leash she was gonna give me."

"Me too," Bill said, "And I got hungry after seeing the doctor."

"That's not a surprise either."

"Stopped at Umpa's and Marsha was there working. Your name came up, and she said she hoped to hear from you or see you."

"Now that is a pleasant surprise."

"Don't ask me what she sees in you, Roger."

"I like cats and dogs. I take them in, you know."

Bill said, "Yeah, you look like a stray in need of rescue. Clean up and take a bath before you see anyone, especially certain women we know."

"Quite your exaggerating, Bill .I didn't get a bath yesterday, but I can't smell that bad, really."

"Goatman said there was a foul odor he noticed about your property as he passed, like something dead. He asked me to check it out, and I now know the source."

"Bill, you really know how to hurt a guy, you do."

"Take a bath, Roger. Oh, one more tidbit of info. Don't know if it will help or not, but Missy had a nipple ring. Don't know if that was in the report you have or not."

"No, it wasn't. Could be useful. You never know."

"Any more info or insults Bill, ole buddy?"

"No, the beer's gone, and that's my signal to get back to work."

"Don't let the door hit you on the way out."

"I won't. You never know what kind of mischief and/or mayhem is going on that needs my professional attention."

"Yeah, you probably need some sack time with Connie," Roger said. "Don't give me that innocent look. Remember her? The gal you sent me to for information we needed on the Windover case?"

"No, that old cougar will leave you worn out, scratched, and bleedin'."

"That why you sent me to her without warning?"

Bill said, "It was more like a vaccination for you, Roger. Now you know what's she's like and should have immunity against her charms."

"I'd rather just had a warning. What if I'd been interested

in what she was peddling?"

"Yeah, that would have been interesting."

Roger swore under his breath.

Bill said, "Sounds like my cue to leave. Call me when you have something and aren't so grumpy and take a bath too. Hernandez wants to talk with you, too."

Roger said, "Think I need to train my dog to attack annoying people on command."

"No way. Me and K9 are buddies, ain't that right K9?"

K9 showed her teeth and growled, but didn't open her eyes or move. "See, Roger? What did I tell you?"

"I think it's in your best interest to leave now, Bill. I may be the one doing the biting."

"Very well and remember, you're talking to an officer of the law," Bill said.

"You won't let me forget that sorry fact. I'll call you when I get around to it."

"Call, but see the others first. Could be important. Bye."

Bill left the house, walked to the truck, and soon disappeared.

Roger sat and grumbled to himself. Bill knew how to push his buttons. He needed to hide them more. He figured he knew what Hernandez wanted. So far he had free reign, and he hoped it continued. What information if any did the preacher have? He smiled as he thought of Marsha. He hadn't thought much about women since his wife had died. Maybe he should. Marsha could be a good start, maybe. Definitely not Connie, the man-eater. He had a feeling things were going to get interesting for him in more ways than one, and his feelings were seldom wrong.

# CHAPTER 20

"Well, Mr. Smith, that sure was fun. Let's do it again soon, real soon."

Mr. Smith smiled. "Yeah, it was. How about now?"

"Later, Mr. Smith. Later."

"Mrs. Smith? It's later."

"So it is, but we have business calling. The D or someone lower in the delegation will be calling soon. It's unlikely they'll want us to drop everything right now and go, but it could happen."

"Mrs. Smith, there's not much more we could drop right now." He lifted the sheet and looked at her naked body next to his.

She smiled, "Yeah, I guess there's not, but I don't want to be the one to have to face the wrath of the order. They'll be plenty of time for more fun in the sack. You don't think I keep you around just because you're tall, dark, and handsome and can lift heavy items and reach things up high, do you?"

"I thought it was all that plus my ability to cook."

"That too. You can heat up my oven anytime, but duty calls. You know how it is in this line of work."

"You don't have to remind me. We've been fortunate. A lot of people in our line of work don't last long. Even fewer find time for love and even fewer find time for a family."

"So true, Mr. Smith." Her eyes gazed down his body.

"Looks like you're ready to go again, but it will have to wait."

Mr. Smith whined as she rolled out of bed and walked to the bathroom. The door shut and he could hear the sound of water running. His wife would soon be in the shower when the water got hot. Hot wife in a hot shower. Maybe he should sneak in and shower with her. He'd say he was being environmentally conscious, saving water, saving the planet. But perhaps it wasn't such a good idea. He'd seen his wife in action, and he wouldn't make the mistake of startling her. People had done that. A few lived when she wanted them to, but most didn't. She was dangerous, but so was he. In their line of business, you had to be. You had to be smart, too, or you didn't survive. You learned to improvise, and a little luck helped, also.

He quickly dressed and checked the compound surveillance. All seemed in order. They'd spent tons of money to secure this place. Even more so, none but the best trained would see their handwork, and they'd taken still more precautions to thwart any effort of the best trained opponent to gain entry. No system was foolproof, but theirs was second to none. A call came on the phone, but no number came up on caller ID.

"Yes?"

"Secure?"

"Yes. Secure here. There?"

"Also secure."

"L here."

"M?"

"Near."

"Be ready."

"Job?"

"Yes."

"Where?"

"Nearby."

"Involving?"

There was a hesitation. "ODESSA."

An expletive rolled from his lips. "ODESSA?"

"Correct." Nothing was said for a long moment. "Well?"

"Game on."

"M in agreement?"

Mr. Smith heard the shower water being turned off. "A moment," he said. He cupped the phone in his hand over the receiver, rose, walked to the bathroom door, and pecked on it. "Honey, I need to talk with you," he said loudly.

"Okay," she yelled.

He opened the door, and the steam in the room hit his face. "It's important."

She pulled the curtain back far enough to reveal her face. "A job?"

"Yes."

"Where?"

"Nearby."

Her eyes showed some surprise and concern. "Involving?"

"ODESSA."

"ODESSA?"

"I'm in."

She nodded. "We're in."

"We're in," he said into the phone.

The voice in the phone said, "Affirmative. We'll be in touch. Be ready."

He slipped out of the bathroom and sat at the desk as he finished the conversation concerning a minor detail he needed to be clarified. He sat at the table thinking deeply for a long moment and felt an arm slide around him from the back. He tensed, but knew he was at someone's mercy. Someone licked his ear. "I have you just where I want you."

Mr. Smith relaxed. He knew the voice cooing in his ear. "I was hoping it was you, Mrs. Smith."

"You'd be dead by now if it wasn't."

"You always moved silent as a stalking feline. It's no wonder you got the nickname, The Cat. Teach me some more how you do that."

"I will. And honey, it's later."

He turned to face her. She held a towel to cover her. It dropped to the floor. "Oh my," he said. "My prayers have been answered. Why the change of heart?"

She sat on his lap.

"Oh my, you smell good," he said. "Fresh from the shower and what's that pleasant scent? Channel No. 5?"

"Close but no cigar. It's ylang-ylang. I picked it up while in the Philippines."

"It's heavenly and makes me desire you even more." A lusty growl came from his throat.

She began to unbutton his shirt. "Actually the ylang-ylang flower is what makes Channel No. 5 so sensuous and expensive. You know me. I'm too cheap to pay for that when I can get the same thing for less. And why the change of mind? Well, I'm a woman, and we can do that when we want. Also, we got the call. We have a mission. It's close by, and we have some time.

And it involves ODESSA."

"We nearly died in the last encounter with them."

She continued unbuttoning his shirt and began to unfasten his pants. "We did. I'm female, your wife, I love you, and we could die very soon. Let's make the most of today, husband."

He smiled, and she stood up as did he also. His pants and shirt dropped to the floor. As he picked her up, a little squeal of anticipation slipped through her lips. He carried her to the bed, laid next to her, and pulled up the sheets. "Mrs. Smith, are you ready for some undercover work?"

"Ready and waiting."

"I have a question for your first. Why did come to me wearing a fancy towel and not the regular towels."

She frowned. "The decorator towels are special and not for regular use. Don't you see the difference?"

"No, not really. A towel's a towel."

"It's a little touch that makes me feel more feminine. With the line of work we're in, it makes me feel better, more delicate, more ladylike."

"Don't think I'll ever understand women."

"Nor I. You know the old joke about God, a man wanting a bridge to Hawaii, and trying to understand women."

He nodded. "I do. Tell you what, next time you surprise me dressed only in a towel, use the fancy one again."

"Why? You already know what's under the wrapper."

"I do, but a fancy covering does make the gift package better. I think I' beginning to understand."

She smiled. "I'll take that under consideration. So, is that why you only use those old cloth towels when you're done tinkering around with your gadgets, MacGyver."

"It is. Dirty jobs need old cloths and special events need fancy towels, right? And when did you find out about the MacGyver label? How long have you known my nickname?"

"Awhile. You're always improvising like he is except you use guns and kill when necessary."

"True," he said. "And I'm not a big fan of boats or water. You're much better at that."

"Honey, what are you waiting for? Enough talking from those sweet lips of yours. Kiss me, before I'm forced to attack you again."

Their bodies were soon entangled. Twenty minutes later, they lay in bed side by side. "Mr. Smith, I can't get enough of you. The thought of dying makes me want to live more and love you more in the time we have. You know what I mean?"

"I do, but there are some things worth dying for."

"Agreed and stopping whatever plans ODESSA has is one of them," she said. "Honey, are we REDs?"

"Not yet, but soon I believe. We'll know when the time comes. Retired, Extremely Dangerous, REDs. The time will come. We're set. Financially, we're very well off. Most of the people in this line of work don't live this long."

"So what do we do in the meantime?"

"What we usually do. We wait. We're kinda like firemen. It's mostly looking over your shoulder waiting for something to happen, but in our case, we're on the front line. The fire's already going somewhere, we can be proactive, and light backfires, and put the active fires out."

"Mr. Smith. I love it when you wax poetic."

"Mrs. Smith, I thought you only kept me around for my body."

"That too. We are the good guys, right?"

"We are and when I quit believing that, it will be time develop a plan for an exit. I know some are only in it for the money, and some have flipped, but yes, I believe we are the good guys."

"Agreed. And we wait?"

"We wait until we hear or see more and I think I have a fair idea of where we should be watching?"

"And where might that be?"

He whispered something in her ear.

"I thought so," she said.

# CHAPTER 21

"Hey, Pastor Phil. There's a fellow here says he needs to talk with you. Says he's a friend of Bill Kenney."

"Bill Kenney?" A pregnant pause followed. "Lola, tell him I'm on the phone. Could take a few minutes. Tell him he can wait or make an appointment."

"Okay, Pastor. I'll do that."

The slim woman with a full head of bushy hair came around the corner from the hallway. "The pastor says you can make an appointment or if you have the time, you can wait. Shouldn't be too long."

"I heard and I'll wait."

"Okay, take a chair. Got a pot of coffee over there. It's fresh. Pastor runs on coffee. His last name should be Duncan." She pointed. "There's sugar and creamer in the cup next to the pot if you need it."

"Thanks," Roger said. "I like mine black."

He poured himself a cup full in a Styrofoam container and took a sip. "Hey, this is good. Tastes like medium roast. Just like I like it."

She smiled. "Can't say I've ever seen you around here before, Mr. Pyles. Are you new to the area?"

"I am. I've been kind of a homebody since I moved here from up north. I hadn't gone out much till recently. It feels good to stretch my legs a bit, you know?"

"I've lived here all my life. My family moved here long ago. I'm sixth generation Florida Cracker. They came shortly after the Seminoles moved south before the Civil War. None of the family fought in the war. They were too busy driving beef north to feed the Confederate troops. An army rides on its stomach. A soldier can't fight well if he's starving.

"They were here when this place was all open range back when the range wars occurred. Some of my relatives died then. Few people know about the range wars in Florida. Most think of them all as out west. This place sure has changed over the years. Brevard County was a sleepy place till the Space Center was established. It boomed like crazy and then busted after the moon program drew to a close. The shuttle program pulled us out of that, and now it's going strong until the next dumb president pulls the plug for some dumb reason. People need to know how important keeping ahead in space is."

"No argument there, Miss Lola."

"It's Mrs., but you can call me Lola like everyone around here does."

"Okay, you can call me Roger. Just curious, the range wars were a long time ago. How much do you know about those old wars?"

"Some, not much. It was long before I was born. I'm the youngest in my family. My older siblings probably know more. My oldest brother is 31 years older than me. As I said, I don't know much, but I do remember as a young child when the subject came up, the room got quiet and the conversations were in hushed tones. Best I could figure out, some of the wounds were still fresh, and no one seemed to want to stir things up again. I think some of the descendants of both families are still deeply involved in Florida politics and many would like to keep things quiet. Let sleeping dogs lie, they say. If you asked me, I'd say there are some things that happened in the past, people would like to keep buried and forgotten. That's my opinion for what it's worth. Why do you ask?"

"Just curious. I ran across something at the dig up at Windover outside of Titusville."

"Now, I know why your name and face are familiar. You're the fellow that was involved in finding the killer of the young woman at the dig into that old Indian burial site. And then you were involved when Stiltsville down in the Indian River behind here blew up and burned down. It was all over the local paper, *Florida Today*. Did they get the story right?"

"Yeah, that's me. Did they get it right? For the most part, yes, but there were some omissions."

"That's pretty normal and about what I thought."

They heard a door hinge squeak, and a voice called out, "Lola, did he stay?"

"He sure did, Pastor. Is it okay to send him back?"

"Sure is. Could you get me a coffee too?"

"Sure will, Pastor." Lola looked at Roger and said to, "Looks like he'll see you now." The phone began to ring, and she said, "Would you get him a cup and take it back? He likes it black like you do."

"Sure thing."

Lola answered the phone, "Hello, Riverside Baptist Church. Can I help you?"

Roger watched as Lola tensed up. He could tell it wasn't good news. Quickly, he got the coffee. He could see Lola wildly scribbling away on a notepad. She only repeated "Ah ha," as she wrote. Her voice was tight and lines formed on her face. It was definitely not good news and seemed to be getting worse as she listened.

He turned the corner to the hallway to the office. Roger's hands were full of coffee cups, so he said, "Okay to come in?"

"Sure thing."

Roger pushed the door aside with his foot and placed one cup before the pastor. "She got a phone call and asked me to bring this to you."

"And you are?"

"Name's Roger Pyles."

"Thank you for the coffee. I'm Pastor Phil Nassey. Bill Kenney said you possibly would be showing up."

"I should have known. Old Bill's quite a rascal."

"He is. He sometimes shows up for services. I know he's no saint, but saint or sinner, all are welcome here. This church is a hospital for the hurting and the sinners. It's not a museum or mausoleum for the saints."

"Aren't the latter often called the frozen chosen?"

"They are. We have a few of those like any church does. We even have a few hypocrites, too."

"Really? Most places wouldn't admit that," Roger said.

"We're not most places. We deal with reality and it ain't always pretty."

"Yeah, I think your secretary just got one of those not pretty calls. She looked concerned."

"Yes, we've had more than our share of trials lately. Mr. Pyles, you're quite welcome to attend any time. And if you're going to let a hypocrite stand between you and God, it just means the hypocrite is closer to God than you are."

"Call me Roger. That's a good point. I hadn't thought of it like that. Interesting. I thank you for the invitation and the coffee."

The Pastor said, "What was it you're here for today?"

"Bill told me you possibly may have some information

about a case I'm working on. He said a local doctor may have passed something unusual on to you. Know anything about that?"

"I possibly believe I do. Give me a minute."

The pastor rose from the chair and went through the door to the secretary's desk. Roger could hear them talking, but couldn't make out what they were saying. Roger sipped at his coffee and studied the many books lining the room. The pastor was either well read, or a collector of books, or both.

A long minute late, the pastor returned. He shut the door behind him and said, "It was bad news, very bad. One of our senior members who's been undergoing cancer treatment was on his way to the clinic with his wife driving. A car crossed the medium on US 1 down in Cocoa and hit them head-on. Neither survived."

"I'm sorry to hear that."

"Terrible news. You never know when your world will end or be turned upside down."

"How well I know that."

Pastor said, "Lola's notifying people and looking like I'll be officiating a double funeral sometime soon."

Roger bit his lip as a wave of grief hit him. How well he knew the shock and pain from losing loved ones.

"Are you okay, Mr. Pyles?"

Roger let out a long sigh and nodded. "Yes," he said unconvincingly. "What was this information you have that could help me? And it's Roger. Mr. Pyles sounds so formal."

# CHAPTER 22

The pastor sat down. "Lola's a great secretary. Sometimes I ask her to sit in on these discussions, but the fewer people who know about this matter, the better. I always ask her to sit in when there's a woman present. You can't be too careful. There are women who would love to accuse you of doing something and ruin you and this church's reputation. It's just the corrupt and fallen world we must live in."

"I can understand that. You can't be too careful. I've heard Billy Graham never is with another woman alone and always has his hotel rooms checked first for women planted there to cause trouble and ill fame to him, his family, and his ministry."

"That's all true. In this case, the information I give you is in confidence. It's all true, but you can't say you got it from me and especially not from the doctor. It's crucial. It'll have an effect on your case, but if you need it to build a case against someone, you'll have to figure out a way to get the records without mentioning either of us."

"I understand," Roger said. "Troubles at the front door so if I need to, find the back door and use it. Are you gonna tell me where the key's hidden?"

"I already have. Figure it out."

Roger's face showed surprise, but he said nothing. He knew the pastor was walking a fine line and there were landmines everywhere capable of taking out all in the vicinity. Roger said, "So what is it you can't say?"

"You're investigating the Missy McCoy murder. Missy grew up in this church. Her parents still attend every week. They were pretty strict with her as she was growing up. We had a band, and she was the drummer and a good one at that. She was a good kid, but she had a streak of rebellion in her. She left home after graduation and traveled with a rock band, I can't remember the name, Heart or Head or something like that, some body part it was. They were making money and building a following, but the drugs, sex, and rock and roll were taking a toll on her. She knew she was going to end up dead if she continued down that path like so many others."

"How do you know this information, Pastor?"

"She told me shortly before her death."

"Go on."

"While she wasn't following the straight and narrow path, at least she was no longer roaring down the highway to hell in the fast lane. She came back to the area, did some crazy stuff that drove her parents bananas though they never stopped praying for her or lost all hope. Missy got married on a whim. She was very impulsive and just as quickly realized she'd made a big mistake. They both wanted the divorce, but there was a lot of shouting, and hard feelings especially from her ex and I believed what she told me on the matter. She hadn't been feeling well for some time and finally went to the doctor. It was obvious something was wrong, but it took a fair amount of testing to figure out what the problem was pancreatic cancer."

"She was kind of young for that," Roger said.

"She was, but it's not unheard of. The worst news was yet to come. It had already advanced to Stage 4 and metastatic."

"How bad had it spread?"

"It was bad. It was in her lymphatic system and throughout her body. Her only hope was chemo or radiation treatment, and her chances on that were less than one percent. In plain English, she was dying, and the cancer was spreading rapidly."

"How long did the doctors give her?" Roger asked.

"Three to six months at best, no more."

"Did she tell anyone?"

"The only people who knew were her parents, her doctor, and me. She told no one else. Her plans were to work as long as she could at her job and quit when she could go on no more. When she talked with me, she was getting ready to quit soon, and then she got murdered at the Canaveral Diner."

"So you're telling me Pastor, she was already a dead woman. If the killer had waited a little while longer, nature would have taken her out."

"That's correct. She had a death sentence. She was a dead woman walking."

"Did Bill know this?"

"No, she was going to tell him, but she found out about his tomcat ways, and their last time together ended in a big confrontation over that. The issue of cancer didn't make it to the table that day."

Pastor Nassey said, "I talked to her on several occasions during this time. She said the realization she was going to die very soon overwhelmed her and it was Bill who took her wrath."

"Hell has no fury like a woman scorned," Roger said.

"Yes, she felt she and Bill had something special and when she found out he was playing the field while they were together, she lost it."

"Do you think Bill could have held it against her and killed her?"

"I don't, but I'm a former cop, and I know that when love and/or alcohol's involved anything's possible. Still, my bet would be on someone else but Bill, for what my opinion is worth."

Roger studied the pastor's face. It showed no guile. "She told you all this?"

"She did. She knew she was dying and she remembered what she'd heard in this little church about God in Heaven, Jesus, and salvation. She thought she'd live life to the fullest or what the world calls the fullest, and then do the Jesus thing, her words, not mine, later in life. When Death stared her in the face, she did some real soul-searching, saw what she needed to do all along, and gave her life to the Lord. She said He was welcome to all she had left. She laughed at that. She didn't have much left, but it was all she had, and she wanted to give it all to Him and live for Him in the fullest. Sounded to her like she was getting the better part of the deal by far. She did, but it ended even before it should have."

"So our killer killed a dead woman," Roger said flatly.

"He did, but her spirit was alive inside, and now she lives with Him forever. That's the silver lining in this cloud. Her death was not the end of the story."

Roger said, "I know about death and where you're going with that. Is there anything more you can tell me that will help me find her killer?"

"My bet would be on the ex."

"There's a motive, but no proof," Roger said.

"You asked my opinion, and you got it. Hope something in what I've told will help you find her killer, bring justice here on earth."

"I hope it does." Roger repeated, "I hope it does," with more force the second time.

"Good. Now the big question."

"Go ahead, Pastor."

"Why are you doing this?"

# CHAPTER 23

Roger said, "I hoped I there'd be some info that would help me on this case. You never know when one little thread will lead you to an entire clothing factory so to speak. I think you've given me another missing piece to the puzzle. I just need to figure how it fits in the whole picture. But I believe there's more to that question, isn't there?"

The pastor smiled and nodded.

"Did Bill tell you more than you're saying, Pastor?"

"Not really. Sometimes ole Bill's a real talker. He's got a gift for gab."

Roger rolled his eyes. "Tell me about it." His voice was a mixture of irony and sarcasm.

"I see you are more than acquainted with Bill."

Roger said, "Correct. We grew up together in West Virginia. After Bill left for Florida to live with his dad when his mom died, I hadn't seen him until recently. He got me involved with what became known as the Windover Case. Like to got me killed, but the strange thing was the case made me feel alive again."

"I've heard of it. It involved Stiltsville getting blown up and burned to the ground, didn't it? How did it make you feel alive, Roger?"

"I had a purpose. Even though it nearly killed me, I had a reason to live."

Pastor Nassey nodded, "Yes. People have asked the question throughout the ages, Why am I here? What's my reason for being? We all need purpose and routine in our lives. What's your purpose and routine like?"

"Can't say I've got much of either. I empty bottles containing alcohol while feeling sorry for myself. Don't think's that really why I'm here. How's that for an honest appraisal?"

"A little more honest than I'm used to, Roger. With a lot of people, you have to drag it out of them if they'll admit to it at all. I like an honest man."

"I'm feeling rather lonely too. Since my wife and son died, it's not been easy."

"The sorrow of losing those important to us can be overwhelming."

"Tell me about it, Pastor. Before I met my wife, I was never lonely. I had a good job and lots to keep me busy. My life was involved in my own pleasures. I enjoyed being a big man on campus. There were lots of good times, parties, adventures, and women to keep me busy. Seemed like I lost everything I valued all at once."

The pastor said, "Loneliness is a terrible thing. Death, divorce, loss of purpose, betrayal, rejection will do it. Loneliness is no respecter of persons. Even our Savior knew it. The Bible tells us, 'He is despised and rejected by men.' Adam and Eve knew it when they sinned. When God asked, 'Adam, where are you?' God knew where Adam was, but did Adam know where he was? The Samaritan woman at the well drawing water who met Jesus sure knew about loneliness. Her choice of lifestyle caused her to be an outcast. The apostle Paul sure had reason for despair. He was stoned, shipwrecked, and nearly beaten to death more than once, yet he endured the hardships of life because he knew in God's economy the best was yet to come. I don't understand why people have to go down in the valley before they can scale the heights, but you have to come to the end of 'self' before you begin to live. The happiest day of my life was when I realized I couldn't make it on my own ability. My mourning was turned to joy, and my sighing became singing. Happy are they that mourn for the inadequacy of self for they shall be comforted by the endless sufficiency of the Lord.

"There was a woman who used to attend here. She moved to Melbourne, so I haven't heard from her in a while. Anyway, she went through a bitter divorce, and their young daughter ended up in a local children's home. The girl felt abandoned and oh so lonely. Her mom only came once a month, and she rarely saw her father. It was years later the girl found out the home only allowed one visit a month, but her mother came every day and stood at the fence hoping to catch a glimpse of her child. God's like that, always there watching even when we can't see or feel His presence. God's active in your life, Roger, whether you know it or not." The pastor stopped. "Tell me, how do you see yourself? What's your greatest asset?"

"Pastor, I like to think of myself as a thinker. I've seen so many people swallow everything that comes down the pike and literally gets swept away in a flood of stupid."

"Tell me about it, please"

"It was one of the things that's so helpful in my forensic work, the ability to see through all the garbage messing up the scene. But it can get you in trouble. Can you believe I was removed from my college teaching position because I was teaching the students to think for themselves?"

"I can. Thinking is dangerous to those who want the perception to be viewed as reality."

"I was always good at ferreting out fact, but it was my late wife who opened my eyes to so many things."

Pastor asked, "Would you care to tell me about it?'

"How long have you got?" Roger asked.

"I was working on Sunday's sermon, but it can wait. Please go on."

Roger said, "Okay. I had my professor job at Western Maryland University. Like I said, I thought I had it all. You know, big man, big title, and lots of girlfriends that come with it. I met Kay at a football game mixer sponsored by a Christian group on campus she was affiliated with. Surprisingly, the two of us hit it off and really enjoyed each other's company. She knew about my reputation with women and told me if I tried anything funny, it was over. I never had a woman talk like that to me before, and it was somewhat of a shock in this day and age, but I respected her for being so honest and candid. She had great faith and lived it. I watched and learned much from her.

"We'd been together for some time, and it was going fine. After a trip to France involving my work, she fixed a big dinner for just the two of us, you know, candlelight and fine china. I brought a bottle of wine back, and there were two things I didn't know. One, she had a weakness for wine and two, this was no ordinary wine. It was more like sherry. The alcohol content was almost 20%. We woke up the next morning in bed together. She told me not to expect any more nights like that, and I knew she was telling me the truth.

Roger continued, "All went fine. Two months later, she tells me she's pregnant. Even though the circumstances were less than ideal, I asked her to marry me, and she said yes. Her mom was concerned about this unequally yoked Bible teaching, but there is another about a husband being justified by a believing wife, so that's how we started."

"Yes," Pastor Nassey said. "I know what you're referring to. It's covered in the books of First and Second Corinthians. You seem to know some scripture."

"I went to a country church growing up," Roger said.

"When I got to college, I put it behind me. Kay brought it all back in my life and challenged me to search for myself and make up my own mind. I liked that about her. She was my rock when the college was unfairly trying to get rid of me.

"I eventually left the school. The whole situation had created a big headache for them. The alumni weren't happy, and word got to the press on how I was being railroaded. The administration offered a large settlement if I would go away. I was going to fight it, but then Kay and our son were killed. It knocked the wind right outta me, and I took it and left the area hoping to put the pain behind me and start over."

"How's that going, Roger?"

"Not very well. I've spent my time drunk and depressed. I wish it had been me that died, not them. I wasn't there when they needed me most."

Tears formed in Roger's eyes and one flowed down his face. He looked at the Pastor. "Bet you must think I'm a real loser."

"No. What I see before me is a hurting man, a man who has endured a lot of pain. A man trying to cope as best he can."

Roger looked past the pastor and said, "We are all travelers in this world, from birth to death, we travel between eternities."

The pastor's face tightened, "What an incredibly powerful statement. What great philosopher wrote that?"

"Don't know. It was a line of graffiti on a concrete retaining wall on my old campus where I taught. Yeah, it's powerful. That's why it stuck with me all these years."

"A sentence like that could carry an entire book or movie, Roger. Mind if I borrow it and use it in a sermon?"

"Nope. It left an impression on me. You know, the last time I talked this much about something like this was with a local rabbi."

"Wouldn't have been Rabbi Katz over on Merritt Island would it?"

"It was."

"He's a good man. We disagreed on some things, but he's the kind of guy you would trust to guard your back in a foxhole."

Roger said, "I had that same feeling about him. He seems to be a very caring guy."

"He is. Funny you should mention him. I had lunch with him at Umpa's recently."

"Bet it was bacon and eggs."

The Pastor laughed. "Eggs, but no bacon or sausage for him. He does try to keep some resemblance of kosher I believe."

"Do you understand kosher?" Roger asked.

"No, and I've asked him in the past to explain how they figure what's kosher and what not. He looked at me surprised and perplexed and said that the leading rabbis are not in agreement on this so I shouldn't worry my Gentile brain trying to figure out what they can't." He paused. "I almost forgot. He mentioned your name and something about something called ODESSA. Does that ring a bell?'

"Yes, ODESSA's an organization that officially doesn't and never has existed, but many believe has and does exist. They supposedly were responsible for getting many of the high ranking German Nazi officials out of the country after the war and are trying to quietly recreate a new Third Reich. Did he say anything else?"

"He seemed alarmed at the news he had, but didn't elaborate on it further."

Roger said, "I may need to talk to the good rabbi." He stopped. "I've taken up too much of your time. I should be going."

The pastor said, "I can make time. I have a few more questions."

"Okay, but it's now on you if you're late for something important."

"That's an easy cross to bear. My first question is about your spiritual life. How is it? How can I help?"

"I should have known," Roger said.

"I'm a preacher. What did you expect?"

"I know. Preachers got to preach, laborers got to labor, carburetors got to carb, and pistons got to..."

"Do what they're supposed to do," the pastor said. "I know that old Pete Seegar tune. He was one of the founders of a group called the Weavers. He wrote lots of songs."

"Yeah, he did. 'If I had a Hammer; Turn, Turn, Turn!' and others."

"Don't forget, 'Where Have all the Flowers Gone?'"

The pastor said, "Like his singing, but don't always agree with his politics. I saw him perform locally with Arlo Guthrie, Woody's son. Arlo lives in Indian River County, the next county south of Brevard."

"Small world. Pastor, you asked a very personal question, and I'll answer you. My wife was the believer. Me, I'm a seeker. I seek for truth and understanding. I learned so much about faith and Christianity from my wife and her church we attended. I'm open to hearing both sides. Some told me I should curse this God who did this to my family, but I can't buy that. This world is full of evil. The human race is capable of doing great things and great self-sacrifice, but it can also do things so wicked it's almost unbelievable."

Pastor Phil said, "I've seen it first hand as a pastor and

cop and serviceman. You live in Canaveral Flats, right? Have you met Rusty Bentley who lives there?"

"Can't say I have."

"He's an ex-Marine who turned missionary, and he worked in some of the worst hot spots in the world doing what he could to help local people, some Christian, protect themselves from government-sponsored marauders, terrorists bent on rape, enslavement of women and children, and killing."

"Pastor, I don't think there is such a thing as an ex-Marine. I do believe Bill may have mentioned him once."

"Good point. I believe he'd be a good person for you to meet."

"I believe so too, pastor. Tell me, are there any normal people living in Canaveral Flats? It sure seems to have its collection of interesting and colorful characters."

"You're the first normal one."

Roger laughed, "Then they better keep on looking if anyone thinks I'm normal."

Pastor Phil laughed too. "Now, that's funny. I'm goin' to have to get busy. Can I say one last thing before you go?"

"Sure."

"Stop in when you can, Roger. Let me know how things are going. I hope you find the killer and lastly if you need to talk on spiritual issues or others, my door's always open. I know you know John 3:16."

"Doesn't everybody? Here's my take on it. God sent His Son into the world to save mankind, each and every one willing to become His children and followers."

"That's the picture, Roger. You'd be surprised the Biblical ignorance creeping into this nation. John 3:17 continues on with that same thought and hope. Jesus gives us hope to carry on in this messed up world."

"Thank you, pastor, for your time, advice, and information. By the way, what do you think of dreams?"

"Why do you ask?"

"Pastor, sometimes I feel a presence, and it gives me comfort. I like to think it's my wife, but it could be God, or both. I had another thing happen last night, not sure what it was. Something I can't explain. The best description I can come up would be to call it a dream. I think I saw a glimpse of Heaven. I saw a misty place and as I watched a huge library full of books going on endlessly appeared. I saw a person standing, and as I was drawn closer, I saw it was my late wife. A young boy was standing next to her. I think it was my son, but her face was the only one I could see clearly. She had a book open in her hands. She looked at me, and she smiled. Then the vision faded away. What do you think of that? She loved books."

"Honestly, I don't know."

"Most people have a hard time admitting they don't know, Pastor."

He nodded. "Was it a vision of Heaven or just something your unconscious brain wanted and created? I'd like to think it was the first and the room was where God keeps all the wisdom and knowledge in the universe available for His children. I think she was smiling because she could see you and she was in a place where all the questions she had ever had could be answered. That's what I think."

Roger said, "I'd like to believe that too. My heart felt like a heavy burden had been lifted when I woke, but it's come back with time."

"I understand. It's like eating and bathing. Got to put good stuff in and wash the bad stuff that builds up away daily."

"Good point, Pastor. I must go."

"Stop in anytime. You're welcome here, Roger."

"Then it's till next time."

"Anytime, Roger. Anytime. My door's always open to those truly in need. Remember, Roger, there's none so damaged that he cannot be fixed by the hand of Almighty God. God loves you. His love for us imperfect and fault-filled people is matchless and too big to be measured. It lasts a lifetime and beyond that. You're His one of a kind wonderful masterpiece that cannot be replaced. He always has His eye on you.

"And one last thought for you, Roger. There's a reason the rearview mirror is so small, and your car's windshield is so big. Hindsight is always 20/20, but you can't drive forward looking back in the mirror. Where you're going is a lot more important than where you've been. Cherish the old memories, but you have so much opportunity to make new ones. Think about it."

Roger acknowledged the profound statement with a little smile that turned into a small grin. "Thanks, Pastor. I will. I appreciate your kind words and encouragement." He walked out of the room, down the hall, and passed the empty secretary's desk and chair. He guessed she was away on church business or in the bathroom. Either way, he let himself out and walked to his vehicle. He heard the roar of traffic from US 1 and could smell the exhaust from the vehicles, both diesel and gasoline. The steering wheel was hot to the touch. He rolled the windows down and sat thinking. Sweat quickly appeared on his face. A frank talk with a man of the cloth always left him with much to think about. And then there was ODESSA. How he hoped he'd never hear that name again. He needed to talk with several people, and one was a murder suspect.

# CHAPTER 24

Sweat rolled down Roger's face and back in beads as he waited for Bill to open his door to his house. A trash can full of garbage not having a lid reeked foul odors, and some flies had managed to get inside the screened porch and buzzed around the putrid banquet.

Roger pounded on the door again. "Come on Bill. Open the door." Roger wiped his brow and swatted at a pesky fly. He saw Bill's face at a nearby window for an instance and then it disappeared.

The door opened, and Bill said, "Well, look what the cat drug in. Come on in, Roger. No point in spending more time out in the heat than what you have to. Come on in. What do I owe the pleasure of your company here today?"

"Give me a beer, you big lug, and I'll start the spiel."

"Okay, don't get testy. I shoulda known this wasn't a social visit."

Bill grabbed two beers from the refrigerator and handed one to Roger. Two psshhhhh sounds followed as the boys cracked the cans. "Ahh, good stuff," Roger said as he wiped the foam from his overgrown mustache.

"Yup, it is. Hits the spot on a hot Florida day which is about every day." He looked at Roger. "You quit shaving? Your mustache gets any longer, and you'll look like a walrus. Quit shaving again? Becoming a filter feeder like some of those whales?"

"You really know how to make a guy feel welcome."

"And what woman in her right mind would want to kiss that?" Bill asked.

"Got a date with Marsha. Hey, it's worth a walk through the forest to get to the picnic. Some welcome I'm gettin' here."

"I did get you a beer without complaining about your showing up unannounced, you know."

"I guess you did. You're a good one to talk though. This place is a pig pen. Don't you ever clean up? I thought the flies on the garbage can outside were going to carry me away. How do you let things go to pot so fast?"

Bill grunted. "No, I'm not much of a housekeeper. Lester's wife used to clean up this place for me and my dad when she was alive. When she got sick and died, his sister took over that job and has been doing it ever since. She's been feeling poorly lately, and the cleanup job ain't been getting done on a timely basis. It's hit or miss with her now."

"There's dust everywhere."

"Roger, you are dust and will return to dust. That's why I don't dust. It could be someone I know."

"What about Lester's sister? Doesn't she have a problem possibly dusting someone up?"

"I guess not. Don't think she knows 'em."

Roger shook his head. "They'd have to fumigate this place before they burned it for health reasons."

"You're a good one to talk. Now, what do you want? I've got places to go and things to do like saving this little town from all kinds of evildoers."

Roger took another sip and slapped his knee. "Like arrest a couple little boys taking keychains from Miller's store?"

"They were ten and should have known better. Mrs. Miller saw one of the smaller boys take some. She reported it to me. I know the boy's family. Good people. I confronted little Johnnie. His mommy was standing right next to him. He blurted out and confessed he had taken two after seeing the older boys take a handful. Well now, we had a major crime wave going on in Canaveral Flats to deal with."

"I bet," Roger said.

"I found the older boys, two brothers, and after a little probing, they confessed too. Promised never to do it again. Got about half of the keychains back. They sold the rest to friends at school. Mrs. Miller didn't want to press charges, but wanted something done so to make up for the trouble they caused, so the boys are doing some painting and weeding and grass mowing for her," Bill said.

"Sounds like you have it all under control. All's well that ends well here in Mayberry, right Sheriff Andy?"

"It worked out to everyone's satisfaction 'cept maybe the boys who had to work off their dirty deeds, Roger"

"Guess so. Crime doesn't pay. Kids need to learn that at an early age."

"I think their daddies whipped their butts too. That'll leave an impression on you."

Roger said, "I remember a few I got. Probably should have got more. Only one I didn't deserve was when my sister got mad at me and lied to our parents about how I broke something she actually broke. They believed the sweet little girl over the big nasty boy. Can you believe that?"

"I can. The female of the species doesn't usually lie as much as men. Men tend to tell lots of little lies, but when females lie, they tend to be bigger and more hurtful. As a cop, I'd say about a quarter of the rape, and domestic accusations were nothing more than a vengeful, lying woman trying to hurt a man badly. They play up the poor little woman against the evil big man. "

"The female of the species is more deadly than the male. Rudyard Kipling said that too."

"So he did, Roger. I think I heard that recently from someone."

"Just the same and in all fairness to my sister," Roger said, "I did get away with a bunch and tormented her a lot, so overall, I can't complain too much about my parent's fairness, or lack of it."

Bill asked, "So what was it you came over here for? Certainly not to play health inspector and complain about my housekeeping or lack of, or the latest crime spree in town, the battle of the sexes, and definitely not to confess for your childhood sins. Why are you here?"

"I have some questions."

"Spit 'em out, or forever hold your peace and go away."

Roger looked Bill directly in the eye. "Did you kill Missy McCoy?"

# CHAPTER 25

"Did I kill Missy McCoy? I'd have thought you'd know the answer to that question by now," Bill said.

"Quit evading my question and answer it. And why no alibi? This would be so much easier for you if you'd tell me where you were the night she died."

Bill's eyes stared right through Roger. "FYI, I did not kill Missy. And the alibi? As I told you, I have my reasons. You'll figure it out eventually."

The two men looked at each other like two alley cats ready to fight. Gradually, Roger's face softened, and he sucked out the last of his beer. "Got any more?"

"You know where they are. Get one for me, too."

Bill slipped into a chair as Roger went into the kitchen and returned with the beers. He gave one to Bill. "Thanks," he said.

Roger took a seat opposite Bill and said, "Now we have that out of the way, what's new that I need to know about?"

"Well, my friend, I got a call from the governor's office. There's been some opposition to the governor's request for money for a professional dig at the Windover site. Some of it's the usual. You know, there're some people in the legislature that hate the governor and will oppose anything he proposes even if it benefits the state and them."

"Think we have some jerks like that in every organization," Roger said.

"Very true. I think sometimes he rattles their cages just to hear them howl like rabid dogs. I believe he enjoys it, but the real sticking point is the bones and carbine you, me, and Tom Kenney found before the pump broke over at the Windover Dig."

"How so?" Roger asked.

"That requires some Florida history. The Civil War may have officially ended in 1865, but the hard feeling and fighting didn't. There were two powerful families in this area, both had land and cattle. It was all open range at that time. One family was pro-Union, and one had supported the Confederacy. Both families were involved in politics in the area and had influence. One family claimed the other owed taxes on cows to their county and took some of the other family's cows as payment. Threats were made, and the sheriff of the county who was a member of the first family was ambushed and killed. A feud broke out."

"Kinda like the Hatfields and McCoys up in the Appalachian Mountains, Bill?"

"You got the picture. The feud escalated into what we know today as the Florida Range War. Over 22 men died before it was over."

Roger said, "I thought all the big range wars were all out West like in Texas or Lincoln County, New Mexico."

"Most people know very little about the history of this state, especially that time period."

"So what's this forgotten piece of history got to do with us today?"

"Roger, those two families are still involved in Florida politics and aren't really interested in having old wounds opened. Better to forget and move on. Governor's trying to convince them it would be better to officially bury the hatchet and support this dig, use it as a teaching lesson on the state's history going all the way back to ancient times."

"Do you think he'll be able to do it?"

"I do. He's a pretty slick operator. If he can't win you over with his goodwill and a smile, he's been known to do some serious arm twisting."

"I see, and he knows where the skeletons are buried. Pun intended," Roger said.

"He does, and Roger, he mentioned he's interested in having you as a part of this project. Maybe even head it up. He's got some people at the state universities interested in being a part of this, and they may fight to do it all. He thinks because you were there from the beginning and are an expert in the field, he can see you have a big part in this, if you're interested."

"Does day follow night? Of course I'm interested. Does a pig love slop? You tell him that. I could call him and tell him so."

Bill said, "I'll call his office and let them know, and I'll leave out the part involving the pig slop. If you know how complicated Florida politics can be involving the locals and people from up north, it would be best if I handle this."

Roger said, "I'll agree with you on that. By the way, I was at a local roadhouse and bar having two or a few and two guys got into a fight. I only heard their conversation when it got loud. One said, "This is how we did it up north." The other yelled, "I don't care how you did it up north," and the fight was on."

"I can believe it."

"By the way Bill, Big Red's back in town."

"Big Red? Can't be." Bill's eyes grew large. "No one from the Sheriff's Department has called about any disturbances and for me to come and arrest him."

"They won't be calling."

"How do you know this?"

Roger gave Bill a pompous smile and said, "I'm kind of a detective, you know and besides, I talked to him after the fight," Roger said. "He's the bouncer at the place now. After they got in a few punches on each other, he grabbed both of them and threw 'em both out in the parking lot. Told 'em to finish it up out there if they wanted, but they looked at Big Red, decided it was a bad idea and shook hands. When they tried to go back in, Red told 'em no, maybe next week, but not tonight. They got in their cars and left. After the place settled down, I ended up next to him at the bar, and we had a good old conversation and time."

"Go on. I'm all ears."

"He told me the bar got tired of him getting in fights with the customers and they worked out a deal. The only fights he would be in would be as bar bouncer, and he could drink all the beer he wanted for free. He said they'd been better off paying him by the hour."

Bill nodded in agreement. "He can drink a lot of beer. Did my name come up?"

"It did. He asked me if I was a friend of yours. I wasn't sure it'd be a good idea to admit to that, so I said you were an acquaintance. He smiled knowingly and told me about the history between the two of you. He said he'd cleaned up his act since he found a steady girlfriend. Said before they all got tired of him, but this one won't leave and is working on rounding off his hard corners."

"Well, good for him. And her. The right woman can do that to a man. I wish him luck."

"He said he wants to talk to you," Roger said.

"What about?"

"He didn't say, but it did seem imperative."

"Nothing more?" Bill asked.

"Nothing more. Guess you'd find out when you see him."

A puzzled look came to Bill's face, and Roger could tell he was thinking of the possibilities. He looked at Roger. "Hernandez has been calling you. Says you never answer your phone. Told me to tell you to call her pronto."

"Hmm. Ain't had any calls for a day or two. Maybe the phone's got problems. I'll check and then call her."

"She seemed pissed. I'd do it real soon, Roger, if I were you."

"Okay, will do. And one more thing, I found a rattlesnake in my mailbox today. You know anything about how it got there?"

Bill's eyes widened, and his eye browses rose. "I didn't till now, but I once found a turtle on a fence post. I think the turtle and snake both had help getting there. Give me all the details. Did you look for evidence on who put it in there?"

"Of course I did. No unusual tracks, car or human in the washboard sand of the road or nearby. And I don't think we'll find any unusual fingerprints on the mailbox. Check with the mail carrier on when she last put mail in the box."

"Can do. Start in the beginning," Bill said.

"Well, I went up to check on the mail, something I don't do every day. When we, the dog and me, got to the box, she began to growl and bark at the box. I thought I heard a buzzing sound inside, so I took a stick and opened it. The snake came flying out of it like a jack in the box. It flew through the air, landed on the road, took off for the nearest ditch, and that was the last I saw of the old unhappy snake. I'm glad K9 was around. She saved my bacon again."

"Seems she did. Were there any other witnesses?" Bill asked.

"No. Hey, you're not insinuating I made this up, are you?"

"Well, let's look at this story, no collaborating witnesses except a dog and no snake. What would you think Mr. Gottahaveproof?"

"I see your point. Just the same, Bill, someone put a snake in my mailbox and tried to cause me bodily harm."

"If the snake bit you, it would have probably gotten drunk and then died."

"Ain't funny, Bill."

"Okay, I believe you. Never known you to lie to me. Who would want to do something like this to you?"

"Well, I guess it could have been some kids," Roger said.

"Could have, but they usually destroy the mailboxes with ball bats or cherry bombs," Bill said. "That kinda died out when the kid blew his hand off some time ago. Probably not kids. You could have made some enemies or someone is trying to send you a message or both."

"That's my thinking, but who and why?"

"Let's think on it and see what we come up with. Do you want to file a police report, Roger?"

"No. I'd rather keep it quiet for now. I think it's best if I don't and only you and me know."

"Whatever you say," Bill said.

"And one more thing before I go. I think it best if you don't leave town till I get this wrapped up.

Bill rolled his eyes. "Whatever you say, old buddy. Guess I'll have to postpone my trip to the inaccessible jungles of the Congo. Might be good for you to stay close also. I'll see you later. Don't let the door hit your backside on the way."

Roger grunted, "Think I better be watching my backside.

See ya."

Bill nodded, "Yeah, I think that would be a good idea. Take care, ole buddy."

Roger grunted again and left. Bill looked out his dirty windows at the departing Roger. K9 sat in the truck with the windows rolled down. She yelped happily when Roger got in. Her eyes saw Bill peering out at them, and she showed her teeth. Roger's eyes followed her gaze, and he saw Bill. A curt smile came to his face followed by a scowl. The truck turned and disappeared from view.

Bill put his hand to his jaw and stroked it several time. Things were getting interesting.

# CHAPTER 26

Roger drove his vehicle up the street where Jim Odom lived. It was an older section of town where the wealthy had once lived, and it seemed many still did. The street was wide and had many large stately oaks growing along it. Their limbs often touched in the middle of the road. He parked beneath one covered in green resurrection ferns. Recent rains had brought them back to life.

He shut off the engine and studied the house. Not one you would expect a killer to live in, but what did your typical murderer's house look like? It was made out of wood and painted mostly white, but the gingerbread trim was decorated in a contrasting color that complimented the house. The finishing boards were all done in an old-fashioned time and labor-intensive way. The windows were painted in a third color that gave the house excellent eye appeal. Someone knew their colors and how they accented each other. He noted a more modern looking barn-like structure behind the house. A marshy area was to the far side of it. Roger wasn't sure if it was a part of a swamp or somehow connected to the nearby Indian River. There were two gates in the ornate woven wire fence around the property, one for pedestrians with a walkway up to the front door and a second for vehicles. The driveway split. One side led to a small garage on the left, and the right side led back to the larger structure.

A well-manicured yard with several flower and herb gardens surrounded the house. Roger looked for evidence of a dog, but saw none. The last thing he wanted was getting bitten by a sneaky dog hiding somewhere as he approached the house.

A thud on the windshield started him. He watched the acorn remains bounce to the hood and then disappear over the side. "Squirrels, most worthless animal in Florida aside from palmetto bugs. Glorified tree rats with a good publicity agent," he grumbled to himself. "Dumbest too. Never can figure out which way to go once in the road. Right, left, right, left, THUD." No wonder they're always lying dead in the street. At least the ones up north were big enough to eat, especially the fox squirrels."

As he got out of the car, a salty breeze from the Indian River brushed his face. The smell of rotten river grass and dead fish found his nose. He wondered if the town of Titusville was still dumping sewage into the lagoon. He hoped not, but anything was possible. Central Florida was sure a beautiful area, but like everywhere on this planet, the effects of human activity, good and bad, could be seen. Mistakes had been made in the past, and it would take time and millions of dollars to try to fix, but it could be done. He'd seen the progress being made in the Potomac up home. Maybe one day it would again be clean enough to swim, fish, and boat in. Fortunately, the Indian River had never gotten that bad, and he sure hoped it didn't.

Roger opened the gate, took a second look for a dog, but again, saw nothing suspicious. He walked up the flagstone walkway, took two steps up to a porch that pretty much wrapped around the whole house. His mind's eye imagined some older people dressed in their Sunday best swaying back and forth in a glider and fanning themselves in the days before air conditioning. The house looked to have been built to make the best use of natural air flow with the widow's walk area at the very top of the house. There was no doorbell, just a large knocker which he used. He heard someone coming over creaky floors. The door opened, and a large deeply tanned man, six foot three or so, wearing a muscle shirt that accented his broad shoulders and thick arms answered the door. He looked at Roger suspiciously. "Yes?" he said.

"I'm Roger Pyles, the police agent investigating the death of your ex-wife. I'm here on the appointment the sheriff's department arranged."

"Then, please come in and accept my apology for not greeting you property. You didn't look like Jehovah's Witnesses, no Watch Towers to sell, or Mormon missionaries, no bicycles. I thought you may be a door to door salesman. Sorry, please come in. You're late."

"I am. There was some kind of parade going on in the old downtown area. There was probably some back way to get here, but I'm new to the area and still discovering the alternative routes."

The man smiled. "Yes, the city's trying to revitalize the historic area. Parades are one way to get people back visiting. My family was among the early settlers to the area when the fishing was excellent, but the mosquitoes would carry you away. The locals have their own club called the Mosquito Beaters, though I've never been to any of their meetings. Where're my manners. Come in." He opened the door and put out his hand. "My name's James Odom, but most people call me Jim or Big Jim."

Roger shook his hand and said, "I can see where the Big Jim name came from." Roger looked at the massive biceps and wondered about possible steroid use. "I have some questions for you about the case. Where would be a good place to do this interview?"

"The kitchen table would work well. You could spread out any notes or papers you have on the case there. Good place for taking notes too. Care for coffee? I brewed a pot of Jamaican Blue Mountain a while ago. I thought you would be here sooner, but I can make a fresh pot if you like."

"Thanks, it will be fine as is. Can't say I've ever had Blue Mountain. I've tasted some exotic blends while doing archaeological work overseas, but somehow missed this one. Liked about all of them, even the one made from beans that went through a jungle cat's guts. Only one I didn't care for was when the locals mixed the coffee with cardamom."

"Very well. Come with me." Jim led Roger through the old house. It was spotless. Everything had a place and was in it. You could have eaten off the floor it was so clean. The only pictures he saw were of a man and a woman both of whom were dressed in clothing fashionable after the Civil War. They had sour expressions on their faces.

"Have a seat," Jim said and pointed to a chair at a table. It appeared to have been the original that came with the house. "I'll get us both a cup."

"Thanks. Do you mind if I tape this meeting?"

Jim hesitated for a moment as if the idea didn't sit well. "No, go ahead. I have nothing to hide." He poured the coffee in a china cup, placed it gently in front of Roger, then got himself a cup, and sat down at the small table across from Roger. "Where do we start?"

Roger put a folder of notes and papers on the table and looked up friendly like, but also firmly. "In the beginning," Roger spoke into the microphone with the usual information needed to start: Where, When, Who, and Why they were there. "Mr. Odom, tell me about yourself and your family. You have a magnificent old and beautiful house. How did you come to own it? Have you been in the area long? I'm sorry if I may ask a bunch of questions that may be obvious, but as I said, I'm fairly new to the area and need some background."

Big Jim began, "My family history in the area goes way back as I mentioned. This was my great grandparent's dream house. They had an interesting history too, but I won't bore you with it. I acquired the house after my parents' deaths about a decade ago when they were killed in a collision with a semi carrying grapefruits on the way to a local packing house that closed recently. I was their only child. Their fortunes went up and down on a seemingly regular basis. It was on a down point when they died. I used their life insurance policy benefits to pay off the debts on the estate. When the dust settled, all I got was this old house and a closed down little theme park south of town."

"That wasn't the place called Tropic Paradise possibly?"

"It was and is. It has something to do with how I met my ex-wife, but let me tell you about the old theme park and my story will make more sense to you."

"Okay, go on," Roger said.

"The park was every kid's dream place to have growing up. It had an Old West town called Dodge City they patterned after the TV series Gunsmoke, which was popular at the time. It had all the characters and of course a Long Branch Saloon, but no alcohol, but they did have shootouts and hangings every hour. Marshall Dillon every day would bring justice to the blackhearts who were always dry-gulching some innocent family or cowpoke. It also had an Indian village, boat and train rides, food, gift shops, lots of animals, and other fun stuff. People loved Monkey Island. As I said, it was a great place to grow up in.

"Like everything else in this state, it had its booms and busts. During one of the downturns, Johnny Weissmuller endorsed the animal theme park, and things picked up again. He lived in central Florida and would be at the park on a regular basis doing appearances and sign autographs and pictures."

"Johnny Weissmuller? You have to mean the fellow who was Tarzan?"

"One and the same, Mr. Pyles."

"This area does have a lot of history."

"It does, and some of it's not so pretty," Jim said.

"What area doesn't have some unpleasant history?"

"True, Mr. Pyles. Anyway, it was some past history that soured my parent's relationship with him. Weissmuller was a world-class swimmer. That's how he got the Tarzan part in the movies. My mother was also a world-class swimmer. What most people don't know is there was a four-minute nude swimming scene in one of the Tarzan movies that never made it to the final cut. Maureen O'Sullivan was the actress in the film, but my mother was her stand-in double for that scene. When my father found out about it, he was shocked. My mother had never said anything about it. My father became suspicious there might be more to the story, and their relationship with Weissmuller went south rapidly. He pulled his support because of some alleged charges of animal treatment. And it didn't help that during one of the numerous after-hours events, an elephant got loose, found her way to US 1, and was struck and killed by a passing truck.

He continued, "Not long after that, Disney World and Sea World opened up in nearby Orlando, and it was all steady downhill for my parents' park. My father turned the trained dolphin loose in the Indian River. People have told me he's still out there dancing on his tail. The monkeys found or made a hole or both and escaped into the surrounding woods. There's a gas station up the road now used for repairing buses. The guys have to lock up their lunches or the monkeys would steal them."

Roger stopped him. "This is all well and good, but how, if at all, does it relate to this case?"

"I was getting to that. My parents were nudists as was Johnny. Some of the regular events held after regular hours were adult in nature. I learned a lot about human behavior long before I should have." He stopped. "How does this relate to the case? I used to frequent the nude area on Playalinda Beach out on the Canaveral National Seashore."

"And Missy was a nudist?" Roger said.

"Correct. I met her during a volleyball game. I spiked the ball. It was a perfect set up, and it drove her to the ground. She fell flat on her back legs flying, and I fell in love right there. We all helped her up. It knocked her silly. They sat her in a folding lawn chair to recover. I told her I was sorry and talked with her as she pulled herself back together. We spent the night together, thought we were in love, got married, and soon found we had very different ideas on our relationship.

"She kept wanting to do skin movies and go to the nudie beach. She said the money was good and she couldn't see the harm in showing off and using her attributes. I wanted it all for myself and no more showing off all her skin to the whole wide world. There were some other things too, and our love soon turned sour. She left, and I was glad to see her go."

Roger said, "I see you have a deep tan. Do you still go to the nude beach?"

"No, I haven't been out there since she left me. I have a little private place I go now and sun my buns out of the public's eye."

"So Jim, who do you think killed her?"

Jim folded his arms. "Well, it wasn't me. I wanted her gone and got that. That cop was a suspect, no? He had motive. I know your report must show they had a nasty breakup just a few days before she was murdered. We'd been divorced for some time, and I'd moved on. My money's on the cop. They know how to kill and get away with it. I heard there was another suspect or two, but they really didn't tell me much for obvious reasons. And I had an alibi. The cop didn't."

"That's interesting, Jim. Tell me, what do you do for a living?"

"I'm a timekeeper for PLE Supplies in Cocoa. Before that,

I was their star salesman. I was tired of the travel required in the job. They didn't want to lose me, so they offered me the time-keeper position. I've been doing that for years now."

"As I said, I'm new here. What does PLE Supplies do?"

"PLE stands for Police and Law Enforcement. We can supply anything they need from clothing, radio equipment, batons, tear gas. You name it, have it in bulk. We supply all the local agencies, many statewide, and some federal agencies I know you've heard of and maybe some you haven't."

"You're still working there?" Roger asked.

"Yes."

"Do you have any objections to me contacting them?"

"None. You'd do it even if I said no, correct, Mr. Pyles?"

"If I felt it's necessary. I've always made it a practice of following the scent trail wherever led me no matter how faint it was. I've solved some cases everyone had given up on and turned a few slam dunks on their heads by catching something others missed. No brag, but I'm very good at what I do. I think this case is nearing a conclusion."

The muscle-bound man's controlled face let slip a look of surprise, but the soon recovered. "That's good news. It will be good to have the whispering voices stop. This chapter needs to finally close."

Roger nodded. "That's correct. I've got enough information for today. I'd like to quit now and possibly get back with you soon if need be. Is that good with you?" Roger could see this sudden end disturbed the other man who tried not to show it. Jim responded, "If you think it best. I was expecting more. My time is valuable, but I would be agreeable to seeing you again. Call first. I have a life to live, and you could show up to an empty house."

"I'll try to do that. Thank you." Roger shut off the recorder, grabbed up the file he'd laid on the table along with the recorder, and rose to his feet. "It's been a pleasure talking with you. Also very insightful. I got what I wanted today, and as I said, I may have some more questions for you soon. Thank you for the great coffee and seeing me on this short notice. I too look forward to the putting this case in the Closed Category Box. I'll find my way out, thank you."

Roger exited the house at a leisurely pace. His eyes scanned the rooms and hallways on the way out. He opened the front door and turned to see Big Jim right behind him. "Oh, you surprised me," Roger said casually. "I just thought of one last question."

Big Jim's face showed some concern. "What? What do you need to know?"

"What was the elephant's name, the one that died in the highway?"

A look of relief came to Jim's face followed by something that appeared to be puzzlement. "Ellie, her name was Ellie. Not very original, I know. Why do you ask the elephant's name?"

"Have you ever read any Agatha Christie, Jim?"

"Only a little I was forced to in high school. Can't say I do much reading."

"She wrote mysteries about crime. One of her characters was a stuffy little Belgium gentleman named Hercule Poirot. He was always talking about using his 'little gray cells' on his cases. The little grey cells of my brain were talking to me. They said that I should ask that question so I did and now I know her name was Ellie. Thank you."

Roger saw confusion on the man's face, but he did nothing to answer the questioning look. "Goodbye," he said as he shuffled on to his vehicle and got in. Jim was still looking at him from the doorway. Roger tapped his head imitating the little detective further. He gave a knowing smile to Jim, waved, and then drove off.

Jim responded with a half-hearted wave as he watched the vehicle disappear. He shut the door and locked it securely. He walked into a dimly lit small room that had the curtains pulled and unlocked a chest. Then he pulled his shirt off, folded it neatly, and laid it on a nearby chair. After placing a necklace around his head, he touched the human nipples, his souvenirs, from his activities. As he read from his journal on the table, he remembered how he had gathered each one. His hand went into his pants, and he began to pleasure himself. They were all starting to run together in his mind except for the first and the latest. He'd had fun with all them, the living and the dead. This nosy cop must be dealt with. Jim had never had sex with a man, living or dead. He wondered what it would be like. This man convinced him he wouldn't stop searching for answers until he had them or died trying. Maybe he could see that both happened for Roger. And why had he asked about the elephant? What had he been trying to tell him? Why did he ask about that he wondered as he stroked his own little trunk? How much did he know? A plan came to him as he climaxed. This man knew too much. He must be dealt with, soon.

# CHAPTER 27

Roger pulled up to the closed gate in his vehicle. He got out and walked to it. The number on the metal warehouse building said 8743, nothing more. This had to be the place. He knew he'd followed the directions he'd been given to the letter. A fence surrounded the entire property, building, and an empty parking lot. He heard a voice call his name. "Roger Pyles."

He yelled out, "Yeah, that's me. Where are you?"

"I've been expecting you." Roger now knew the voice was coming from a speaker on the side of the building. "I'll open the gate, and you drive through. Park in the lot, nose to the fence. The door marked Employees is open. Come on in and up the stairs to the office where the large window is. I'll meet you there."

"Roger that. Roger do." Roger chucked to himself. "I always wanted to say that."

Roger got back in his car, the gate opened, and he drove in and parked. He walked in the building and saw the office at the top of the stairs. He could see a man sitting at a desk near the large window that overlooked the warehouse interior. As he climbed the stairs, a door swung open and a huge man stood in the doorway. He said, "Mr. Pyles. I'm Dan Mason. You contacted me and said you needed to see me when convenient, and it concerned one of my employees, Jim Odom. Come on in."

Roger shook the huge hand. Dan Mason had to be 6 feet 4 or 5 and had some of the broadest shoulders Roger had ever seen on a human being. Roger wondered if the man had to turn sideways to pass through some doors. "Pleased to meet you, Mr. Mason."

"You can call me Captain Dan, but it usually gets shorten to Cap'n Dan. It's how I'm known around the area. Welcome to my business. My father started it years ago from scratch and built it to what it is today. We're one of the largest companies of its kind in America."

"Why do they call you Cap'n Dan?" Roger asked.

"I love boats and being on the water. This is the state for it. Lots of sunshine, water of every kind, fresh, brackish, or salt. Rivers, estuaries, lakes, and the oceans. You name it, we got it. You'll have to come along on one of my fishing trips. Always love to have company."

"Thanks for the invitation. I'll keep it in mind. My experience in Florida with boating's been in a john boat on the Indian River where me and another fellow encountered a killer manatee."

"Killer manatee? Sounds like there's a story there."

"There certainly is, but we don't have time for it now. It's long. Some other time, maybe on your boat. Anyway, thanks for seeing me. I told the Odom fellow I'd probably be checking with you. I'm investigating the murder of his ex-wife, Missy. Something suspicious is going on."

Cap'n Dan said, "That happened about five years ago. I remember it well. A cop came around here, asked a few questions, and left. He seemed like he was just going through the motions."

"Do you remember his name?"

"I do. It was Ryder, Mitch Ryder."

"Like the singer? You know, Mitch Ryder and the Detroit Wheels?" Roger asked.

"Yeah, that's why I remember the name, that and my

training at the Police Academy."

Roger said, "So you were a cop?"

"That I was. I was a Cocoa city cop. I liked it, but got tired of some rats in the force. They were worse than the criminals. You knew the criminals were up to no good, but the backstabbing from some of my own boys in blue got to me. Pop's business was growing like crazy, and he needed help running it. I had the experience and knew what law enforcement wanted and needed. I've been here ever since and have never looked back. I'd only been here a few months when Jim Odom's ex was murdered."

"He said he had an alibi."

"Roger, He did. I saw the time sheets for the night shift. It showed he was here doing yearly inventory."

"Any chance the records could have been forged?"

"Funny you should say that, Roger. Maryanne was our only timekeeper at the time. Jim got the second timekeeper position when we put on a second shift. What's really weird about it is she called in about two weeks ago and up and quit like that. I took the call. She seemed troubled and scared. I couldn't get much out of her. No one here saw it coming. Not even Jim. He'd know if anyone would. It was an open secret they were seeing each other on the sly. He pleaded ignorance on knowing anything about her quitting, but I wonder. Something hinky's been going on around here for years. My father wanted to write it off to accounting errors and honest mistakes, but I talked him into hiring an outside firm to look into it. I was going over the report when you came in. Some of it may have been just glitches in Pop's antiquated accounting, but there seemed to be a pattern of inventory disappearing that can only be contributed to shrinkage."

"Shrinkage?" Roger said. "You mean theft."

"I do. Pop and me agreed to have an outside contractor come in and install a state of the art security and monitoring system. They did it about three weeks ago over a three day weekend when no one was here, and no one would be the wiser. It's well hidden. On a good sign, we've had no car break-ins since the fence went up."

"How's the surveillance system working out?"

"Super as far as I can tell. We have everything on video-tape for that time. Pop took a quick look at it and said it was sat-isfactory. He showed me the basics on how to run the system."

"I've got a hunch. Could you find the tape of Maryanne's last day?"

"Sure can, Roger. Come to the back room where we hid all the hardware and monitoring equipment."

They walked into the back room. Several large monitors sat in a semi-circle on an oversized desk. Each screen was split six ways.

Roger said, "I'm impressed, and I didn't see anything here, so you don't have to kill me."

"I wasn't planning on it. Let's see. Here it is." He put the videotape in the VCR player and hit play. It made some noises as the mechanisms kicked in. A picture of the employee entrance appeared on the black and white screen. They watched as the day started. Timekeeper Maryanne came in shortly ahead of the pack. Dan hit another button, and the picture went into fast-forward mode. The machine buzzed as the images sped by. They watched intently.

"Hey," Roger shouted. "Stop right there. You need to back up."

Cap'n Dan hit the pause button and then the reverse. "You see something?"

"I think so. There! Isn't that Jim Odom? What's he doing

there? He works the late shift and the screen time says this video was taken around noon." They watched a little longer. Maryanne could be seen hurrying out to her car and driving off at a high rate of speed. Not long afterward, Jim Odom exited the building at a run. He hopped in his car and also sped away.

Roger exhaled heavily. "I've got a hunch I know what happened to the lady timekeeper. Do you have fingerprints of your employees?"

"We handle a lot of items that are meant only for law enforcement" Cap'n Dan said. "Some of them would be bad news if they fell into the wrong hands. I know there's a huge demand on the black market both in this country and around the world. To answer your question, yes, we fingerprint everyone."

"How hard would it be to get a copy of Maryanne's fingerprints?"

"Not hard at all for me. I know all the passwords for the systems. What do you need it for?"

"I have a bad feeling about this. When me and Canaveral Flats Chief of Police Bill Kenney were coming back from interviewing a witness in the Missy McCoy cold case, we stopped in south Georgia at a Sonny's BBQ for lunch. We got to talking with some local cops, and they mentioned a recent murder. A young woman was found nude, and somebody had cut off one of her nipples. Someone did the same to Missy. The whole thing smells. Could be the same guy and we may well know who it is."

"It will take me a minute to pull the print's up."

"That's fine. I'll call the sheriff up there and tell him to expect a fax with Maryanne's prints. He needs to compare the two ASAP."

Cap'n Dan had a stern look on his face. "I love it when a plan comes together. Use whatever you want. All the equipment you need is in the outer room."

"Gotcha." Roger went to the next room, pulled a business card out of his wallet, and dialed the phone. After a few rings, someone picked up. Cap'n Dan listened to the one-sided conversation. He could hear Roger explain who he was and why he needed to talk to the sheriff immediately. Luck was with them. The sheriff was in the office, and he was very interested in what Roger had to say. He'd touch base with Roger as soon as his people compared the prints.

Cap'n Dan found the prints and set the printer to the highest quality. The printer made a whirring sound, and a paper with the prints was spat out. "Got'em," he yelled.

"Bring'em here," Roger said.

Cap'n Dan appeared carrying a paper with the prints. "Here."

Roger said, "Once I've sent this, I need to go. Got someone I need to corner. How do I let myself out?"

"Press this button under the desk. Hey, I hate to run, but I'm having a colonoscopy tomorrow, and I can feel the laxative trying to kick in right now. It's working faster than they said it would. I'm gonna be on the throne for a while. Let yourself out and call me when you have something new."

"I will."

"Got to go, now!"

"See ya." Roger placed the document in the fax machine and dialed the Georgia sheriff's fax number. It picked up on the second ring and made the chirping sounds peculiar to fax machines. It went through smoothly, and a confirmation notice printed and came out. He folded it and put it in his pocket. He hit the button under the sink so the gate would be open. As he reached the office door, he heard Cap'n Dan shout out in a troubled voice, "Hey, old buddy, could you please do me a favor, please, pretty please?"

"Sure. What do you need?"

"Paper. Toilet paper. Ain't none in here, and I'm screwed. Help me!"

Roger snickered to himself. He bit his tongue as he tried not to make a comment worthy of the predicament Cap'n Dan found himself in. "Where's the paper?" he managed to say without laughing.

"In the closet in the hall. Bring two rolls please."

Roger opened the closet door. To the left he saw a large sealed box labeled, Buns Toilet Tissue, Ultra soft and Gentle on Hemorrhoids, Giant Economy Pack. He tore at the cardboard box top and managed to rip the securely glued and stapled halves apart. Inside he saw the entire contents was enclosed in a thick plastic bag. He fought at it and managed to poke a hole in the bag which he enlarged with some effort. He grabbed two rolls each individually wrapped in fine white paper. He stopped for a moment and looked at the writing on the box. "One may be the loneliest number, but we're here for you with Number Two. We're the butt of many jokes. We won't rub you wrong. One or Two, we comfort you."

Roger went to the bathroom door. "Sorry, it took so long. The manufacturer sure went to great effort to protect the toilet paper. And then the slogans on the box caught my eye. Better than Burma Shave signs." He asked the door, "Now what do you want me to do?"

"Just open the door a little and slip your arm with the paper in. I can reach it from there." Roger did as Cap'n Dan had instructed. "Thanks, Roger old buddy. I owe you a big one. You got me out of a real jam. Thanks. Yeah, someone at Buns definitely has a sense of humor. I've noticed that too." He laughed. "I wish some of our other suppliers were as diligent and meticulous with what they send. You wouldn't believe what some of the stock look like when they arrive."

Roger said, "A company's pride and quality shows in everything they do. Hey, you're welcome. Aren't you kinda young for a colonoscopy?"

"Yeah, I am, but there's a family history of colon cancer. My uncle died from it. He ignored the symptoms and by the time he finally went to the doctor, it was too late."

"Sorry to hear that. Hope you get favorable test results. I'll let myself out. Hope everything comes out okay." He heard a groan. "Colon cancer runs in my family too, so I can relate to what you're going through. I had one of those procedures not too long ago. I wish you luck and good fortune." Roger paused. "I'll let myself out now. Take care."

"Roger, I have a crappy feeling about this. It will end well." He stopped. "Thanks again."

"See ya." Roger made his way out of the office and to the parking lot. A large white panel van was parked next to his vehicle. As Roger got to his door, the side door of the van opened rapidly. An invisible force hit him, and he fell down. As he lay on the asphalt unable to move, he heard a voice, the voice of Jim Odom. "Why, it's just the person I wanted to see, Roger Pyles? We've got much to talk about and so many fun things to do."

Muscular arms picked him up and dropped him in the van. The door closed behind him. He'd been tased. Roger could feel his hands and feet being bound, and he was helpless to stop it. Looking up, he saw Jim with a syringe in his hand. He felt a pick to his thigh. "Don't worry Roger. I've done this before. Only killed one person so far using too much. Elephant tranquilizer can be tricky when given to humans. It's super potent."

"Why?" muttered Roger.

"Why? Because I want to and can. And no one can stop me."

Roger saw an evil darkness in Jim's eyes as he lost consciousness.

"Aw," said Jim. "I hope I haven't killed him. It's too soon. That would cut down on our fun." Roger moved slightly. "Oh good, I love playing with my toys. Use them up while alive and then when they're dead. And then get rid of the trash and find another when it suits me. Let the games begin."

# CHAPTER 28

Roger slowly gained consciousness. His mind was fuzzy, and he struggled to remember and make sense of his situation. He had been drugged, bound, and lay helpless. He looked around cautiously. The interior of the van was covered with what he recognized as sound deadening materials. He guessed that was why he hadn't been gagged. The van swayed. It was moving, and he was the cargo going somewhere to a place he was sure he wouldn't enjoy. He fought the grogginess and spoke to the driver, "Hey."

The driver turned to him and flashed a wicked smile. "Hey yourself. I hadn't expected you to come around so soon. Still got to work on adjusting the amount of fentanyl."

"What's that?" Roger croaked.

"Elephant tranquilizer. Potent stuff. Many times stronger than heroine. You like it?"

Roger's head spun. "No, think I'll stick to killing myself with alcohol. Where are we going?"

"To my playpen."

"Oh. Is that where you took the others?"

The wicked grin on Jim's face grew darker. "Why should I tell you?"

Roger fought for consciousness and blurted out, "Why not? You have me where you want me. You're gonna kill me anyway? Right?"

"You're a smart fellow, too smart for your own good. You could have stayed out of this, and everything would have continued just fine."

"You mean your stalking and killing games, right?"

"Mental note to self, next time use more tranquilizer."

Roger spoke, but he slurred his words. It took little effort to do this. "Why don't you tell me? I'm your captive audience."

A depraved laugh slipped from Jim's lips. He thought for a moment and said, "Why not? What do you want to know. You're dead meat anyway."

"Yeah, why not? You have me where you want me." He paused to gather his foggy thoughts. "Tell me about Missy."

"It's her fault I kill. She was a bitch. I grew to hate her, and she needed killing. I found I liked killing. It's her fault."

"How did you get into the diner?"

Jim laughed. "I duplicated her keys. I could have done whatever I wanted to her and whenever I wanted."

"Why at the diner?"

"Simple. It's the place she'd have least expected it."

"You shot her with a taser?" Roger asked.

"I did. People become really helpless after shot with one."

"I know."

Jim laughed at Roger's predicament.

"Let me guess, you got it from work."

"I did, Sherlock."

"And then what?" Roger asked.

"I wanted to humiliate her, and I did leaving her like that.

She died too soon. It should have been much more fun. I used chloroform, and I used too much. She died quickly, too quickly."

"Why did you stab her twenty-three times?" Roger asked.

"Poetic justice. She betrayed me. Caesar was stabbed twenty-three times. It seemed only fitting."

"What about the others? How many?"

"Prostitutes, runaways, people no one would miss. How many? Too many and yet not enough. I'll count the souvenirs I kept and let you know. I'm still adding to the collection when I need to."

Roger said, "What about Maryanne? Why did you kill her, Jim?"

"We had a good thing going covering each other's secrets. The sex was good too, but she changed. She was tired of pretending and covering up. She said she was going to report me, and my fun had to go on, so I had to take care of her. It was her fault. We could have kept going as it was, but no, she changed and made me silence her forever, but oh, did she squeal. It was so exciting. She had some powerful lungs."

"That's your plans for me, too? Make me cry out for mercy, and then you torture me more?"

Jim's face twisted into a devilish smile. "Something like that. I've never had sex with a man before. I figured I just do the same to you I did to the others. You know, screw you lame, conscious or unconscious, kneeling, sitting, lying down, bent over, standing on one leg. And all the while, I'll be controlling you and choking you in and out of consciousness. You'll be impressed with the devices I've created for my sensual activities. If you could walk later, you'd walk funny for at least a week. Sound like fun, eh?"

For once, Roger was glad he was tranquilized. Roger was looking at a classic case of a predator. It calmed him as he thought of the fate Jim's victims have suffered. He wasn't there yet, and there was still time to escape. All he needed was an opportunity, if it ever came.

"Almost there. Hope you're up for it. I am," Jim said.

Roger could feel the van slow and make a left-hand turn. It went a short distance and stopped. Through the windshield, he could see a chain link fence gate and an old rust sign that read Tropic Paradise. Jim cursed as he looked in the rearview mirror. Roger thought he heard a muffled commanding voice outside and he watched as Jim's right hand reached for a gun on the floor. With all the strength he had, Roger thrashed against his binds and yelled, "He's got a gun!"

Two shots rang out, one immediately after the other. Roger heard Jim moan. Blood poured from his neck. He slumped over in the driver's seat, and his head rolled to the side. Roger thought he heard someone shuffling around outside. He yelled with all he had left inside, "I'm in here. Help me!"

It was quiet for a moment. Roger saw a hand with a gun through the glass in the passenger's door. "Help me, please! I'm in the back."

A face appeared, but Roger couldn't make out who it was. The door window exploded from a hard hit from something. Roger saw a gun aiming at Jim who wasn't moving. The man's other hand reached inside the van, touched the automatic lock, and Roger heard the sound of all the doors on the van unlocking. The side door opened, and Roger was temporarily blinded by the sunlight. "Roger, are you okay?"

The excited voice was familiar. "Bill, is that you?"

"Yes, are you okay?"

"I'm kinda tied up right now, but could be a lot worse. You can't believe how glad I am to see you." Roger turned his head and used it to point to the driver. "Is he dead?"

"I think so. Stay right there while I check to see he's not a threat anymore."

The human mind is a strange thing. The most sarcastic of thoughts sometimes comes at the craziest time, and Roger's was no exception. *Stay right there? Did Bill seriously think he could jump up and run away?* Even with his inhabitations and thought filters lowered to almost non-existent, Roger bit his tongue and said nothing. Bill quickly returned. "He won't cause anyone any trouble anymore."

Bill looked at the expertly tied knots that held Roger. His pocket knife made quick work of them. "Thank you," Roger said. He swung his legs out of the van side door and would have fallen out but for Bill's quick hands.

"Steady, old boy," Bill said. "You act like you're drugged."

"He shot something in me. Said it was elephant tranquilizer."

"I can believe that. Other than that, are you okay?"

"I am, Bill. He had a world of hurt planned for me like all his other victims. Glad you showed up. How did you know?"

Bill started to speak when two county deputies' cars with blue lights flashing and sirens blaring pulled in followed by an equally loud and bright EMT box truck. "Roger, don't go anywhere. I got to explain what's going on to the new arrivals. Fortunately, I'm in uniform, and it will be simpler to explain."

"Okay, old buddy. I'll sit tight while my world chooses to spin now and then."

Bill calmly walked over to the cops who had their

hands on their guns ready to draw. After a quick explanation, the two cops looked over the scene and made doubly sure Jim was dead. They went to their cars, got yellow crime tape, and began to secure the area. Bill spoke to the EMTs and pointed to Roger. Quickly, they went to the back of the truck, pulled out a gurney, and wheeled it to where Roger sat. The older of two said, "Mr. Pyles, we need to take you in for observation and make sure you're okay. Do you understand?"

Roger nodded in the affirmative and the two men helped a very wobbly Roger onto the gurney. Once they had him secure, they wheeled him to the box truck, and put him in. The younger man got in the driver's position while the other went in the back with Roger who lay on the gurney. Red lights came on, and the EMT vehicle took off up US 1. It quickly disappeared.

Canaveral Flats Chief of Police Bill Kenney watched as the truck disappeared with his friend. His thoughts returned to where he was. If not for training, quick reflexes, and a little luck, the outcome could have been very different. It could have been him lying dead on the ground instead of the man in the van. He didn't ever want to think of what could have happened to Roger.

There was going to be a lot of questions and a lot of paperwork before this was over. They'd keep his gun while the investigation was going on. He had others he could use. They might try to get him off his beat, but Canaveral Flats had no policies for its one man force on how to handle police shootings. He wasn't sure how that would work out.

The realization that he'd just killed a man made him sick in the stomach. He felt like a crushing burden had found his shoulders. He'd hoped he'd never have to take another life in the line of duty while he served, but he had a second time. He remembered how he felt the first time, bad, but not this bad. The first time the bank robber was shooting at his fellow cops. This time it was different, just him and Jim face to face. The look on Jim's face told him Jim knew who he was and it was pure hated. It was him or Jim. One of them was going to die, and Bill didn't want it to be him. Fate had smiled on him today. He said a short prayer of thanks to God. He wasn't ready to die.

At that time, he saw the new forensics van pull up. Three people got out. He recognized the coroner and Hernandez, but the third person, a young woman he did not know wearing dark blue pants and a light blue shirt with a county badge. He noted she was tall with a trim figure and well-formed breasts. No, he definitely wasn't dead if he noted them. He shook those thoughts from his head. It was time for clean, undistracted thinking. There was going to be a ton of questions, and he needed a clear head. He hoped Roger was okay. Maybe Roger could tell him who phoned in the tip about him being in trouble.

# CHAPTER 29

Roger walked into the Sheriff's Department Building on Merritt Island. He noted the door glass had been covered with a reflective coating permitting those inside to see out and those outside not to. Charlotte the secretary was sitting at a desk to greet, screen, and direct visitors.

"Why hello, Mr. Pyles. How are you? I haven't seen you in a while. Hernandez said you'd be coming. I'll let her know you're here. You need to wait, okay."

"Okay. Change of procedure? It was just walk on up before."

"It is. We're getting more security conscious. There've been too many instances of bad guys taking advantage of poor to nonexistent security at establishments like police offices, courthouses, and schools and causing trouble. My mommy always liked to say, 'An ounce of prevention is worth a pound of cure.'"

"True. Same reason we have sheepdogs guarding the flocks from wolves."

"Very true. I'll let her know you've arrived." Charlotte called on her phone. Roger could follow the conversation by her actions. She put the handset back on the phone base. "She says to come on up."

"Thanks, Charlotte. How much new security does this building have?"

"I'm not allowed to say. Word gets out too easy."

"Are you packin'?"

She smiled, "I am. What I can say more is that so is about everyone else in the facility. We have a few here, mainly women who are a little squeamish about guns, that aren't packin', but if you knew them, let me tell you, it's better they aren't. They'd be more danger to themselves than the bad guys. The sheriff gave everybody the opportunity for firearm training. Some chose not to take it. Bad guys can get guns. Having a law won't stop them, but a good guy with a gun can. You're a sitting duck without a firearm."

"What you carrying?"

"I'll admit to a seven-shot 9 millimeter."

"Anything more, Charlotte?"

"No comment."

"I don't see the gun. Must be hidden really well."

She grinned, "It is, but I can get to it real quick if I want. Sheriff wants me to get qualified for open carry next. I'm working on it now. Now, why don't you skedaddle on up to Hernandez? She's a busy person and don't like to be kept waiting." She said this in her deepest Southern accent.

"Okay," he said. "I know when it's time to move on."

She smiled devilishly. "It is, Roger. You have a nice day now. Don't get me in 'Bless your heart' mode.'"

Roger grinned back, "No, we wouldn't. Places to go. People to see."

Roger went up the stairs taking two steps at a time. He knocked on the closed door to Hernandez's office. "Come in," he heard a female voice say, and he did. She was writing on an official-looking report he took to be about the Missy McCoy case. "Sit down," she said. "I'll be right with you."

Roger took a seat and waited. The room seemed different. It was. New paint. The old drab institutional green had been covered with a light blue. He liked it. She took the paper she was working on, placed it on top of a short stack, tapped them all on the desk, and placed two paper clips on them to hold them together. "Good work, Mr. Pyles. I'm almost done with the final report on the Missy McCoy cold case. It would have never been solved without you. Try not to get yourself so involved next time. The last thing we need is a death on our hands. You done good."

Roger grimaced slightly. "Thank you. Things don't always go the way you anticipated. There are times you have to take the Bugs Bunny philosophy on life."

"I don't think I've ever heard that. Explain please."

"Whatever hole you pop out of, you have to deal with the situation at hand no matter how unexpected."

She nodded. "I think I understand. If you find yourself in a carrot patch, be thankful for your good fortune, but you need to be careful. The Elmer Fudds and Yosemite Sams of this world may not welcome you and try to send you quickly on your way."

"I think that's it in a nutshell," Roger said. "Like Bugs, I try not to be a one trick pony. I try to have options and if they're limited, make the best of it and hope for an opportunity to come up."

"Roger, from your report, that's a pretty good description of what happened. How did you decide on who Missy's killer was? What gave it away?"

"I came to a conclusion almost from the beginning it most likely wasn't Bill Kenney. His not being willing to provide an alibi was the biggest thing against him. He was holding back, protecting someone and now we know. It came as a surprise to me."

She said, "People have their reasons. Some are afraid to tell the truth because of fear of what another could do to them, and some are trying to protect others. Now we know."

Roger said, "Our killer had to be an oddball. Bill may fit that category in some ways, but the killer was a different kind of an oddball. The killer was a neatness nut. Bill is anything but. Jim Odom fit the bill to a T. When I saw his house, inside and out, I knew he was the one almost without question. Everything was in place, and you could eat off the floor."

"I was there when they searched the dead man's place," Hernandez said. "We found a journal where he recorded everything he did to the women. I've seen and heard of some depraved stuff in my life, but this ranks up near the top. He also had a big box of pictures of naked people. Some were taken at the Tropic Paradise. Others at the beach. The ones from the former appear to go back decades from the hairstyles on the women."

"Do you know who they were?"

"Some have been identified. Others of interest are still being looked into. It seems a lot of the movers and shakers, past and present, of the area are there."

"Was any of them of Bill's friend, Shirley Harden?" Roger asked.

"Yes, just your standard naked pictures for her, but some of the others weren't as innocent."

"Some were of her husband in compromising positions with youths, girls and boys. I need you to keep this under your hat for now. We're trying to find out who the children are. We have a good case against him, but I want it to be a slam dunk. Put him away for years and years. And we now know why the case's investigator did such a shoddy job. We found a picture of him and Mr. Harden having sex. He's going to been fired soon.

"Roger, I wish you could have been there when we did the

searches, but you were in the hospital and now part of the story. It was best for you to be moved aside and me to take it from that point."

"Understood," he said. "And I was in no condition to help. They told me the elephant tranquilizer was something called fentanyl, and it's some very bad and potent juju. I couldn't believe I slept for 24 hours straight at the hospital."

"I checked on you as did Bill. I wasn't familiar with the drug, but the doctors and nurses gave me a crash course. I hope that stuff never makes it into the underworld. All I can see is death and pain in the end. Are you sure your report on how it happened is accurate? It was very detailed without gaps."

Roger said, "I talked with the doctors about that. They said they believed the adrenaline rush in the very beginning helped me remain lucid, but when the threat was over, I crashed. They said they'd seen it before."

She asked, "So you don't remember anything after getting in the EMT vehicle?"

"Just a little. I remember them giving me an IV. I think there may have been a mild painkiller in it."

"The EMT's report says nothing on that, but that's not to say it didn't happen. Things have been known to be left out of reports for someone's convenience."

"True," he remarked knowingly. "Sometimes what's not said can be as important as what is."

"We also searched Tropic Paradise. It's been determined that's where Odom took his victims. He had all kinds of torture devices rigged up."

Roger whistled through his teeth. "A regular Marquis de Sade?"

"Yes. I'll see you get a copy of the final report. The Titusville Police helped us and did an inventory of all of Jim Odom's handiwork. I only saw one personally. It consisted of a barrel lying on its side bolted to the floor. There were straps to restrain the hands and feet of someone draped over it. You can use your imagination on how it was used."

"That's sick and disgusting. And it could have been me he put on it."

"You're a lucky man, Roger. Try not to depend on it in your detective work."

His head nodded several times, and he sighed heavily. "Agreed."

Neither said anything for a moment as it sank in on how close a call Roger had with a depraved killer. She broke the silence. "Overall, I'm very pleased we'll be able to put our first cold case in the closed file so soon. Good work even if you almost got killed solving it. The powers that be are interested in keeping you around. Would you possibly be interested?"

Roger said, "I would if we could work out the details. Right now my status around here is kind of vague. I guarantee I'll do my best if we can hammer out an agreement. And I'm not planning on getting myself killed, but you never know."

She said, "They like you around here. They think you have backbone and tenacity. Maybe a little of a college egghead, but you get results. I'll see what I can do on my end." She stopped. "I have one question?"

"What's that?"

"Any idea on who the guardian angel was who called in about your predicament? The call number to 911 was blocked, and whoever that called garbled his voice. You can't even tell if it was a he. There's no way of identifying the voice or where the call originated. And they asked for Bill Kenney. Somehow they knew he was close. Bill swears it wasn't him that placed the call."

"No," he said. "My gut tells me it wasn't Bill. I'd like to shake that person's hand whoever it was, but I doubt we'll ever find out. Guardian Angels have a way of staying hidden, not showing themselves, but you know they're there. I suspect this isn't the first one I've put in a rubber room in my lifetime. Somehow, I've always gotten out of my jams with minimum damage."

"Roger, I'm not much of a religious person, but somehow I think none of us will die until God in His wisdom, says 'Time's up.' It wasn't your time to die. I'm glad you didn't."

"Me too. I could use a stiff drink."

She said, "I could too, but there's none here. Be careful, I've seen a lot of cops drink their lives away or worse."

"Yeah, tell me about it." He stopped and looked her square in the eye. "Are we done here? Got anything more. I'd like to go."

"I don't have any more questions about this case at this time, but I do have something else, but it can wait for a better time."

"I'm good with that." He got up. "I'm looking forward to the final report."

She said, "I'll see you get a draft before the final report. You can check for accuracy and suggest any changes you feel are pertinent to the case."

"That will work. I'll see you later. Bye."

"Bye," she said and watched as he disappeared from view. She felt exhausted mentally and physically. Her eyes fell on an official-looking manila envelope on her desk from GTR, Genetic Technical Reports that had arrived yesterday. She'd paid for it out of her own pocket. She wanted no conflict of interest by using county facilities to pay the expense.

It was unopened. She'd wanted to open it with Roger present, but the timing hadn't been right. She ripped the envelope edge with a sharp letter opener and pulled out the contents. It started with the usual standard legal speak and went on way too long with possible disclaimers. Some slick lawyer had written it she was sure. She read on line by line until she got to the part she had been looking for. Her breath was audible as she exhaled. Just as she thought.

# CHAPTER 30

Roger's catnap ended when he heard the squeal of brakes in front of his place. He looked up and saw Bill's truck slide to a halt on the sandy washboard road known as Canaveral Flats Boulevard. Bill quickly got out, made his way through the dummy-locked gate, and down the path to Roger's old trailer. As he opened the screen door, Roger shushed him and pointed to the cat sleeping on his lap. Carefully, Bill closed the door making little sound and disappeared into the trailer.

Five minutes later he reappeared. He had a pleasant relieved look on his face and two beers in his hand. He handed one to Roger and took a seat in a plastic lawn chair next to Roger. Bill said, "So how's it going, buddy? You okay?"

"Probably better than I deserve to be. Thanks for not making a commotion. The cat may have found a home, but she can still be jittery. She was in this same position yesterday when an old truck went by. It backfired, and she dug outta here like a rocket taking off at the Cape. I've got the claw marks on my legs to prove it."

"I believe it. You don't have to show me. Told you, you had a cat."

"You told me she had me."

"I did. Either way, you have a cat. Gonna get her fixed, Roger?"

"I will soon. Too many Toms cattin' around. Like to do something about her teeth too. They're sharp. She gives me little love bits. Don't think she means to hurt me, but those teeth sure are sharp."

"Young cat's teeth can be very sharp like all young animals including human. Time will take care of that."

"I hope so, Bill. She drew blood yesterday again."

"How's K9 taking it all?"

"She's okay with the cat, not jealous like I thought she would be. Guess she and the cat are kinda like kindred spirits, two creatures alone in this world."

"Who found you."

"Yeah," Roger said. "They make good company even if they shed."

"Every blessing has its drawbacks."

"Women are like that."

"Yeah, you're right. K9 came through again, she did."

"Yes, she did."

The two men were quiet for a moment. Roger said, "How'd you know how to find me?"

"I got an anonymous call telling me you were in trouble. I stopped Jim's van, and that's when the shooting began."

"What reason did you legally have to stop him?"

"Any officer can stop any vehicle in this state if that officer has reasonable cause as to the vehicle having safety concerns."

"I see."

"Just about any vehicle has some kind of issue and if it doesn't, they may and can develop one."

"Like a broken light?" Roger asked.

"I'd rather not comment on that, but it has been known to happen, so I have heard."

There was a silence between them for a few moments. They sipped at their beers and Roger stroked the sleeping cat on his lap. K9 moved around adjusting herself as she slept. A muffled bark slipped from her closed mouth. The men eyed her. Roger said, "I wonder what dogs dream of?"

"I don't know. Maybe tummy rubs and bones to chew on. Squirrels to chase."

An introspective look came to Roger's face. "Bill?"

"What?"

"Thanks for saving my sorry carcass."

"You're welcome. The good guys won this time. It doesn't always end that way. Wish I didn't have to kill him. He drew on me and took a shot. Fortunately, I was ready. I had my hand on my gun, and as he swung around in his van, I lunged to the right. As I fell, I got off a round, and it found my target. Killing a man's a horrible thing."

"Some criminals don't think so," Roger said.

"I know. The thin blue line is streaked with the red blood of many fallen law officers."

"Guess you did save the county the cost of a trial."

Bill sighed, "Wasn't trying to. Just trying to save myself. Still, if it had gone to trial and he was found guilty and then sentenced to death, it could be decades before he'd be executed with all the appeals his lawyers and the bleeding hearts would throw up as roadblocks."

"Don't seem fair, Bill"

"It's not. Justice delayed is justice denied."

"How many victims do they think he had?" Roger said.

"They're not sure. The nipple necklace he wore had eight nipples on it. At this time, we have to assume he only took one nipple from each woman he killed, not two, but there may have been others where he didn't take a souvenir. We may never know. The nipple in the center of the necklace did have a ring in it. The coroner's doing the best he can to see if it was Missy's. There's been a lot of pretty decomposed Jan Does found in the last few years. Some of them could have been his victims too. We may never know how many. Roger, that sick puppy could have had yours on the string, you know?"

"I do. Glad it's not. Who do you think called in the anonymous tip?"

"I wish I knew. Seems like you've got a guardian angel out there somewhere. If I were you, I'd not be pressing my luck on issues of this nature in the future."

"Bill, you know me."

"I do. That's why I'm giving you this advice you'll probably ignore."

"Thanks, anyway."

"When did you figure out it wasn't me who killed Missy?

"Bill, I had my doubts from the very beginning. I didn't think you had it in you, but stranger things have happened. I had to keep an open mind, and I also had to keep you guessing and see what you'd do. Thanks for not disappointing me."

"You're welcome."

"What was the clincher, Roger?"

"The really odd thing about this whole crime was how the perp left the victim's clothing neatly piled and folded at the scene of the crime. I'm sorry Bill, but you're nowhere close to a neatness nut. You live like a pig. You'd be living in your own filth if not for your housekeeper."

"You don't have to be so hard on me and make it sound so bad, even if it did eliminate me as a suspect. You could be kinder, Mr. College Professor. I know you know how to do that."

Roger gave Bill a dirty look. "Okay, how about this. Bill, your domicile is noteworthy. It far exceeded normally accept standards dealing with lack of cleanliness. You could give professional and convincing lessons to Oscar on the Odd Couple TV show on extreme messiness. You're in the top 1% in the kingdom of Bedraggled. Now does that make you feel any better, ole buddy?"

Awe showed on Bill's face, and then he smiled. "I think I've been insulted."

"Dazzle them with brilliance or baffle them with BS. Maybe a little of both."

"Sounds good to me as long as this cloud of suspicion no longer hangs over my head," Bill said. "Any ideas on what's you're gonna do now that this case is winding up? Word I hear is the powers what be would like you to stay around and help."

"I've been thinking a lot lately. Been rather introspective. I sure miss my wife and kid. They're gone and not coming back. Some lady company might be nice." Roger stroked the cat's head and back.

Bill nodded, but said nothing, however his eyes said for Roger to go on.

"I was wondering about going back to teaching at a college, but I'm not sure I want to. Not sure I could find a place where I would feel wanted and welcomed anymore. I'm too much of a real free thinker ready for open discussion from all sides and so many colleges, and universities have become so closed-minded. Not sure if I could find a place that protects constitutionally protected speech where the First Amendment is respected. A different viewpoint seems to offend some weak people and understanding through looking at all viewpoints doesn't seem to be welcome. This nation's not perfect, but I'd rather be here than any other. I value our culture, as imperfect as it is."

"As long as nations are made of imperfect people, they won't be perfect."

"Very correct, Bill. Censorship only reflects a society's lack of confidence in itself. It's a hallmark of authoritarian regimes like the Nazis, Stalinists, Maoists, socialists, and communists. Tyrants always say they support free speech. They use it to indoctrinate and proselytize, but once they gained control, it became a liability and must be suppressed. I see it happening on today's campuses and fear it's spreading."

"So what's you gonna do?"

"Don't know if I'm up for the fight," Roger said. "I think for now my best place is to stay here and see what I can do with the fresh and cold cases around here."

"Hernandez and others would welcome that. We need all the help we can get."

Roger said, "I'm leaning that way, but I'll let you know for sure. In the meantime, I think I'll stop down at Umpa's Restaurant and see if Marsha is still interested in a try at another date."

"What happened the first time?"

"Nothin'. One of her kids got sick, and she canceled."

"Think the kid was really sick? Not fakin' it to keep some strange man away from his mom?" Bill asked.

"No, she said he was sick. Picked up something at school. Puking all over the place. I think I'll try again. A little time around a good looking and fun lady would be a welcome change from the company who just happens to be drinking another of my beers nearby, Bill."

Bill chugged the last of his beer. "Want another beer?"

"Sure," Roger said. "Get me another one of my Jamaican Red Stripe beers. And while you're at it, why don't you get another for yourself, old buddy."

Bill seemed unfazed by Roger's tone. He flashed a "No worries, mon" smile as he left for the beer. When he returned, he handed one to Roger and popped open the one in his hand. "You sure have a good supply of beer, mon. And nice and cold too, mon."

"You're welcome. Seems you've been a major reason my supply's been dwindling."

Bill smiled, "Ya mon, tanks, no problem."

Roger gave Bill prize-worthy eye roll. "If I didn't have this cat on my lap, I might boot you off my property."

"Don't disturb the cat on my account. She may just dig into a grumpy old man's thighs, and that would only make him grumpier, if that's possible."

"True. Guess you better be going then."

"I will. Till I see you next time. Roger, that Roger. Oh, I made a funny, and the grumpy old man didn't like it."

"Get outta here before I do something I may regret."

"Okay, okay. I know when I've worn out my welcome. Thanks for the beer. Come again anytime."

"Maybe I should throw this cat with the razor-sharp claws on you."

"Don't do it. I'm not worth the effort, and you could be arrested for cruelty to animals."

"True. The cat probably would catch some exotic disease from you, Bill"

"Thanks again, Roger for your wonderful hospitality and the Caribbean refreshments."

Roger snarled.

Bill said, "Okay, okay. I'm leaving."

"Bill, there is one more important thing you need to know. Missy was dying. She'd just been diagnosed with pancreatic cancer. She didn't have long to live. If her killer had only waited, nature would have finished her off."

A dumbstruck look came to his face. "What?" He stumbled for words. "Dying?" He sighed. "That would explain a lot of things. You sure know how to drop a bombshell."

Roger said, "Now, answer me a question. What was your alibi and how was Shirley involved?"

Bill sat back down. "Okay, I can tell you now. I was in bed with Shirley at the time Missy died. It's a little complicated. Shirley and B.J. were married in name only. B.J. was with his boyfriend in Orlando. They stayed together for two reasons: the kids and because they enjoyed the perks of him being a county commissioner. They didn't want news of this to get out, or the good life would be over. They didn't want to spoil the life they'd taken time to build up even if it was a facade. Shirley said she would provide me with an alibi, but I said no. It would work out. I knew it would. Now her divorce is coming up, and the story is known around the county, there's no point in hiding it anymore. Shirley and me were humping like dogs in heat in her bed when Missy died, and that's the truth."

In a neutral voice, Roger said, "I can believe that. It's what I suspected. I had to hear it from your lips."

"It was a difficult secret to keep, but it was my choice. I wanted to protect Shirley as best I could."

"I believe I understand."

The two men said nothing for a moment. Bill said, "Now, I know I have to go. Think I've got some thinking to do. Bye."

"Bye."

Roger watched as he walked down the lane to his truck. He nearly stumbled on the dirt path. Bill looked at Roger, but Roger looked down at the cat and pretended he hadn't seen the misstep. Bill turned back and continued walking. Clearly, Bill's mind was elsewhere. He hopped in his truck. Roger waved as Bill started out and Bill responded half-heartedly.

Roger sighed and stroked the cat's back. "You know, cat. That guy can come through in a pinch, but he sure can be a pain and a surprise too. What do you think of that?"

She turned her head to look at him, stretched, and then got cozy on his lap. "You know, cat, this is the beginning of a beautiful friendship. Now all you need is a name. I'll have to work on one that suits you."

Roger stroked the cat's back, and she began to purr. Roger smiled. Maybe he'd call her Purrfect. He'd think on it.

What was he going to do? Going back to teach didn't seem appealing at this time. The thought of a new minor at a college in female companionship did have a certain allure to it, but he thought perhaps he was over the one night stands and girlfriend flings. Marriage had spoiled him. He wanted and needed commitment.

Maybe he would stay here and continue helping the local law enforcement agencies. What else did he have to do? It'd nearly gotten him killed doing so, but he wasn't drinking as much, and if he continued drinking himself into a stupor every day, he would kill himself. Dying for something he loved and believed in was undoubtedly the better of the two. Maybe he would stay. Maybe. Why not? All he had to lose was his life. But if he did die, it would be on his feet doing what he was good at, not passed out drunk on a floor alone. Yeah, he'd help as long as he was needed and he wanted to. After that, who knows? He'd cross that bridge when he got there. Maybe he'd try beauty school then. He chuckled to himself. Beauty school? Not. Who was he trying to kid?

He stroked the cat's back some more, and she stretched out her front legs so far her claws showed. He heard the phone, but ignored it as it continued to ring. The cat looked up at him as if to ask, "Aren't you going to answer it?"

"No, I'm not, cat. Probably another salesman trying to sell me a cemetery plot or a time-share neither of which I want or need at this time." Roger heard the familiar voice on the answering machine say, "No one is available to answer your call. Leave a message, and it will be returned as soon as possible."

A male voice rang out, "Hey you big galoof. Answer your phone. This is Bill. I know you're there. Anyway, in all the harassment I forgot to tell you some good news. I had another call from the governor's office. Seems a deal on getting funding for a serious archaeological dig at the Windover site should soon be a done deal. A little jawboning and back slapping and palm greasing on some pet projects of some of the opposition by our illustrious governor and voila, the votes are there for funding. Ain't democracy great?

"Oh, there's still some elbowing around for a place at the table by the archaeologists on the state universities' payrolls, but the governor seems very confident he can get all to see it would be best to have the person who did the original investigation as the head of the project. In other words, punkinhead, you've got a job right up your alley if you still want it. It's yours for the asking. And by the way, Mr. Do Good, watch out for the vermin as you drain the swamp. They call it home and fight dirty to keep it dirty. That's all. Thanks for the beer and as Forrest Gump says, 'Have a nice day.' Later gator. Bye."

Roger smiled. Yup, bad things can happen to people with good intentions. It was wise to beware and be prepared. And now some good news from ole Bill. He'd been in need of some, but who was this Gump fellow? Another one of Canaveral Flats' interesting assortment of oddball characters? Roger did remember seeing a book with that name on the cover on

Bill's overflowing coffee table at his house next to another book by John D. MacDonald. Roger knew who MacDonald was. Born in the same general area as he was and transplanted to Florida as he likewise now was. But this Gump guy? Well, whatever. He stroked the cat's back gently. Somehow, he had a feeling it would all work out in the long run. He'd seen it happen in the lives of others. Maybe it was his turn for a revelation.

# CHAPTER 31

"Mr. Smith. I'm home. Where are you?" She sat the full brown paper bag with the green Publix Super Market label on the side on the counter.

A voice came from the other room. "I know. You set off all the alarms on purpose to let me know that."

"I did. I didn't feel like doing a Peter Seller's Pink Panther and Kato routine."

Mr. Smith walked into the kitchen. "Yeah, the last time you did that it was kind of intense. We really tore up this place."

"We did," she said. "Gators been fed lately?"

"Not since the two Russians. Why?"

"They seemed very hungry today."

He said, "Hungry gators make great watchdogs. Fat ones with full stomachs do not. Still, I'll check. Don't want them eating each other." He stopped. "We had a call while you were gone."

"And?" she said.

"It was them."

"And?"

"And they approved of the way we handled the situation and stayed out of it for the most part. We didn't blow our cover, and we protected our subject."

"So what do we do now?"

"We wait and watch. ODESSA is still out there, but our contact couldn't tell us where or when they'll move, so we wait and watch. Report if we see or hear anything helpful."

"About what I thought" she said. "These are the times I hate. I feel like an impatient vulture. I want to get something going. I want to kill something."

"I know. Patience. We wait, and we wait, and we wait some more."

"Right. We wait and make the best of it. Do you think the subject is aware of us, Mr. Smith?"

"No, but I hear he's slick and smart, when he's not drinking his cares away."

"Maybe we should send him a bottle for solving the case?"

"No, Mrs. Smith. I don't think so," he said. "It could make him wonder who sent it and why."

"True. We wait and watch till there's something to report. That was pretty slick how you slipped the snake in his mailbox."

"Thanks honey. It made him up his game a notch."

"Did you tell D about it?" she asked.

"No, it was a detail they didn't need to know." He stopped. "ODESSA's still out there planning."

She smiled, "And we'll be waiting and ready."

"We will."

"Oh, by the way my husband, your father's back in town."

"How do you know?"

"I saw a goat grazing near the front fence."

"Hmmm. That would be a definite sign he's come back.

Guess I'll need to go over and see him. Can't have him coming here."

"No, definitely not a good idea. There are days Mr. Smith, I can't believe you came from that stock."

"Most people don't get to pick their parents. Still, I think I get my sense of adventure from him. It's just directed in a different manner. And doing without when I was a kid, did toughen me up to the harsh realities of this world. You learn to use what you have, to improvise, and make do when you have to. Guess that's where the MacGyver in me comes from."

"True," she said. "I'll take you just as you are. What're your feelings on this present situation?"

"I don't know. It frightens me a little bit. They were and are a ruthless adversary, but something's changed with them, and I'm not sure where it will end, not in a good way I'm afraid."

"There is no good way with them, dear."

"I know. I'm afraid they'll only become wiser and more deadly."

"Husband, I believe you're right."

"So we wait. We listen. We watch. We wait. We try to have a plan ready when the call comes as it will."

"Yes. We'll be ready."

"We will. Not being ready could be fatal," she said.

He nodded. "We'll be ready."

# The End

# WANT TO READ MORE?

*Braddock's Gold Novels – Braddock's Gold, Hunter's*

*Moon, Fool's Wisdom, and Killing Darkness*

*Florida Murder Mystery Novels – Death at Windover and Murder at the Canaveral Diner*

*Murder at the Canaveral Diner* is the second in the expanding *Florida Murder Mystery Novels*. While each book in the series is a stand-alone novel, they're all great stories on their own. Readers say he keeps getting better. All of Mr. Heavner's six books can be found on Amazon as ebooks and paperbacks. The first book, *Braddock's Gold*, is also available as an audiobook from Audible at Amazon.

# WANT TO HELP THE AUTHOR?

If you enjoyed the book, would you help get the word out? Please tell others about it. Word-of-mouth advertising is the best marketing tool on this planet.

A good review on Amazon, Goodreads, or elsewhere would help with the author being able to keep writing full time. It doesn't have to be long. Thanks.

# SIGN UP FOR JAY HEAVNER'S NEWSLETTER

With this, Jay will occasionally keep you informed with new books coming out and anything else special. Feel free to email him at jay@jayheavner.com. His website is www.jayheavner.com. He loves reader feedback.